P9-DET-447

CLARK
COLLECTION I

CLARK COLLECTION I

TIFFANY BELLE CLARK

WestBow Press books may be ordered through booksellers or by contacting:

WestBow Press
A Division of Thomas Nelson & Zondervan
1663 Liberty Drive
Bloomington, IN 47403
www.westbowpress.com
844-714-3454

Clark, Tiffany Belle.
Clark collection I/ Tiffany Belle Clark. –First edition.
x, 230 p. ; 21 cm.
Summary: "Children's stories with a touch of Southern charm that will give your heart a smile."
1. The Holy Bible--Juvenile fiction. 2. Twins–Juvenile fiction. 3. Prayers–Juvenile fiction. 4. Halloween–Juvenile fiction. 5. Singing–Juvenile fiction. 6. Family–Juvenile fiction. 7. Unidentified flying objects–Juvenile fiction. 8. Crafting–Juvenile fiction. 9. Genealogy–Juvenile fiction. 10. Cemeteries–Juvenile fiction. I. Tiffany Belle Clark. II. Clark Collection I.

Aunt Edie, How God Made Twins—1st ed. © 2021
Aunt Edie, Noah's Ark—1st ed. © 2021
Aunt Edie, Spontaneous Creation—1st ed. © 2021
Aunt Edie, First Librarian—1st ed. © 2021
The Halloween Prayer—1st ed. © 2021
The Twelfth Song—1st ed. © 2021
Decoration Day—1st ed. © 2021
Flag Day—1st ed. © 2021
The Floating Light—1st ed. © 2021
Pearl & Pepper Plan Their Year—1st ed. © 2021

Scripture taken from the King James Version of The Holy Bible.

Cover and interior design by Tiffany Belle Clark.

ISBN: 978-1-6642-4747-5 (sc)
ISBN: 978-1-6642-4748-2 (e)

Print information available on the last page.

WestBow Press rev. date: 12/01/2021

Contents

Introduction 1

AUNT EDIE'S TALL SHORT TALES

1. Aunt Edie, How God Made Twins 9
2. Aunt Edie, Noah's Ark 19
3. Aunt Edie, Spontaneous Creation 30
4. Aunt Edie, First Librarian 40

CHANDLER

The Halloween Prayer 53

The Twelfth Song 60

THE DIXIES

Decoration Day 69

Flag Day 73

THE GUMSHOES

1. The Floating Light 83

COUSINS, TOO

1. Pearl & Pepper Plan Their Year 101
2. Pearl & Pepper Redecorate Their Rooms 119
3. Pearl & Pepper Make A Cookbook..... 133
4. Pearl & Pepper In The City.................. 152
5. Pearl & Pepper Make Repairs...............171
6. Pearl & Pepper The Family Quilt 184
7. Pearl & Pepper Crossword Crochet..... 201
8. Pearl & Pepper The Letter Challenge...217

Clark Collection I

Introduction

Each series has its own grace and charm of the South. The characters will touch your heart, delight, and make you laugh.

AUNT EDIE, pronounced Eedee, has twin nieces who want to catch her at her own game. Edie can spin a tale like a weaver with silver thread. Some of the things she comes up with are, some say, farfetched but she doesn't mind. Nobody can prove her tales are untrue and she has dared them to try on more than one occasion.

Edie has gentle brown hair with copper highlights that is long enough to float just below her shoulders though more often than not she wears it in a quickly-drawn-up pony tail that swishes and sways around her head. She dresses casually, usually with a touch of her favorite colors silver and peach.

Edie's eyes glow from an ocean blue when she is deep in thought to a smiling silver when she is amused, triumphant, or teasing. Which she often is!

Her twin nieces have green eyes and coppery brown hair with sandy highlights that shines golden blond in the sunlight.

They prefer to wear snappy, strong colors like ocean blue and apple green. They think this marks them as smart. And so they are. Curious, clever, quick to conclude; and they think, quick to catch.

CHANDLER's Libby is excited about Halloween. She believes it's a day for a special prayer.

Renée's song travels around the world, uniting Christians in praise of our Lord.

THE DIXIES are a Southern family who take every chance they can to be together. Their gentle charm and appreciation for family warms the heart. They love fun, God, and each other –though not necessarily in that order.

THE GUMSHOES' Travis is looking for big adventurer while Lakeland is more practical and Gage is just happy to tag along. These three friends see something in the sky and are determined to get proof of what's up there.

COUSINS, TOO are 2nd cousins who love crafts and family. Once they identify something that needs doing, they set about planning a way to achieve it.

Pearl and Pepper have the same sure gray eyes and black hair. Pearl has straight, chin length hair that swings around her while Pepper's hair lightly curls and bounces.

Pearl is the leader of the two. She comes up with ideas but mostly sees the grand picture and finished product. Pepper, on the other hand, notices details, patterns, and designs with the eye of an artist.

Aunt Edie's Tall Short Tales

Aunt Edie, How God Made Twins

It began one day when Aunt Edie overheard the girls talking about being twins. Though twins are not so unusual, the girls didn't know anyone else who had a sibling that was identical.

It was difficult to have a sister the same age, far more so one who looks exactly like oneself. They went to their Aunt Edie with great concern in their hearts.

"Why did God make us the same? Was he too tired to make a new girl and just made a copy of another one?" A twin asked.

"Why is everybody else one of a kind and we're not? Didn't he love each of us?" Her sister said.

Aunt Edie looked at the two most precious gifts in her life. "Come on girls, let's sit down and I'll tell you how God creates twins."

Edie was a wonderful storyteller and the girls loved to hear her weave and spin a good story, though they had to wonder if her tales were completely true. Some of them were a bit beyond the edge of a cookie.

Once they were cuddled up on the couch, Aunt Edie began. "God is big on planning. He's quite careful about every person that he creates. I believe that he goes back several generations, maybe even a thousand years, on every new soul."

"When God is laying out the plans for a fresh new child, he considers many possibilities. He spins the world around and around examining many circumstances."

Edie patted one twin on the knee. "Making a new soul is quite complicated. Oh, how God loves humans. How intricate, so many layers and depths, how complex. Such possibilities for our existence; for our joy."

One girl squirmed closer. Aunt Edie was so very smart. How did she know all of these things?

"Well, as usual he began to assemble the parts of a new person. First, he needed a body. He started with a lump of clay to fashion the new person."

Eyebrows frowning in concentration, two sets of soft green eyes squinted, imagining God in a workshop molding new people.

"Where does he get the clay?" A twin asked.

"That's right! There's no clay in Heaven," said the other.

"Yeah, the ground is gold."

Edie continued. "He knew that he wanted a particular spirit alongside specific characteristics and, of course, the eyes and smile had to be just so." Aunt Edie swept her silvery blue eyes from one beautiful little girl to the other.

"Imagine, if you will, a workroom. Alphabet style blocks with drawings of families, musical notes, color schemes, and so on stacked one on top of the other in a jumble. There are drawings and drafting plans of people in many shapes and sizes spread out on a grand table in a room that overlooks the earth. What plans and opportunity he imagines."

Edie held one girl's hand. "As he mixed and matched portions of personality and family member blocks, he settled upon two designs of favor."

Her voice lowered to the whisper of a shared secret. "Now, you understand that this happens quite often. Typically, when reviewing his creations, he will look them over and will perceive a preference. The one gets made into a person and the other is returned to the drafting table; maybe to be used in the future."

"On this occasion, however, he liked them both. No matter how he tried he couldn't seem to select one over the other. Well, he doesn't rush through these things and he thought the matter over for some time."

"How long is sometime?" One girl asked.

"Were we already on the way?" said the other.

"Did you know about us yet?"

"I'm getting to that," Edie squeezed their hands, her silver watch tossing a twinkle of light.

Edie took a moment to collect her thoughts. "He visited families and tested out the new humans in one place and then another. The results were mixed but neither were the right fit."

Edie smiled to herself, her ocean blue eyes flashing silver. "He tried something that has worked well in the past. He considered putting one new child in one time period and allowing the other to be born several generations later. You've seen how sometimes a person looks so much like a great-grandparent."

Aunt Edie shook her head. "But it didn't work. The souls simply did not sing in those families or places or times."

"Souls sing?"

"How does that happen?"

"Can we hear them?"

"Do they sing a concert for God on Saturday nights?"

"There is so very much to consider, you know." Edie went on. "And God rarely tosses dice to make his decisions. I would say never, actually." She nodded with satisfaction, her hair dancing.

"Finally, he tried a tactic that always works."

The girls held their breath. This was when they were made. Their whole lives were formed in this moment.

Aunt Edie continued, "God held each of you in a hand, looked deep into your eyes, right through to your soul, and then he smiled at you."

The girls perked up. "God smiled?"
"What did it look like?"
"Were the angels there?"
"When did God tell you all this?"
"Did he smile at you before you were born?"

Edie tried to hide a grin. "As with all souls who receive his smile, you laughed. You laughed of joy and love and delight at who you were; who you are."

The girls were in awe imagining their souls in the palms of God's hands.

"The melody of your souls spilling through your voice and into the bells of your laughter delighted God's heart. He was pleased with what he had made."

"Well, in that moment the creator couldn't, wouldn't give up on either design. They were both masterpieces."

Edie looked from girl to girl. "There was nothing for it. There would just have to be two."

The twins nodded with delight. There had to be two.

"At first he planned to put one over yonder and another over there but what if they ever met? How creepy would that be?"

"That would be kind of weird."

"What if you met yourself while on vacation!"

The girls stared at each other imagining what could have happened.

Drawing them back to her story Edie said, "'No,' he thought to himself. 'They will have to be together from the start.'"

"I couldn't bear it if we were apart."

"Two perfect. Two together."

"We are two."

"It's just like Noah's ark."

"That's right. God loved you so much that he had to make two of you to receive it all."

Hugging them close, Aunt Edie said, "And I'm so happy he did. He didn't give me one blessing, he gave me two."

Edie's heart brimmed with love as she watched her nieces, silver glowing in her blue eyes.

Aunt Edie, Noah's Ark

One day the girls were helping Aunt Edie in her garden. Edie was planting some tulips while the girls played in the yard.

"Aunt Edie? How did all of the animals live in the ark?" They asked.

Aunt Edie looked up from the flowers she was planting. "The ark? As in Noah's ark?"

The little girls nodded. "There are so many animals in the world. How did they all fit into that tiny little boat?"

Edie laughed. "I think Noah would be offended to hear his ship called a boat." She pulled off her gloves and stretched.

"There wasn't room for all those creatures to walk around."

"Did they get seasick?"

"It must have been so noisy."

"Can you imagine the fussing!"

"And just what did they do with all that poop?!"

Edie admired a bloom on a tulip flower, her ocean blue eyes beginning a silver twinkle. "I imagine that they weren't awake to poop—or fuss."

"They weren't awake?" Two little heads swiveled in a single motion.

"They were ALIVE when they went into the ark."

"You can't be saying that God raised them from the dead later!"

"That's ridiculous."

Edie chuckled. "What do bears do in the winter?"

The girls stopped; completely still, as the implications rolled into their minds.

"Once God shut the door," said Edie, patting the dirt around a flower, "the animals bedded down for a long nap."

"Hibernation," whispered one little girl letting the word, the concept, bounce through the air.

"They slept through it." The other crinkled her soft green eyes imagining a boat full of sleeping animals and a few adults playing cards as the rain poured down outside.

The girls exchanged a glance. Well, that explained it. They were sleeping.

As a thought occurred, a small frown furrowed one's brow. "But still, there wasn't enough room, surely," she said.

Catching on, her twin looked at their aunt, confused. "Yeah, there are too many animals on the earth to fit in there."

Aunt Edie couldn't hide her smile. She moved toward the porch swing. "Come here my sweets," she said.

The girls eagerly climbed into the swing. Aunt Edie was going to tell a story. If truth be known, she was famous for them.

"You know that I am not a Bible scholar, though I do have some ideas." Aunt Edie thought for a moment then began to weave a story.

"God is extremely wise. Plus, he has the luxury of time. He can take as long as he needs to think something over, seeing as how he can control time."

"Now, you know that God created all of the creatures on the earth. He knows how everything works, how the tiny little cells in our bodies fit together to make us and all things living and non-living."

The ears of two little girls stood up, their eyes honing to a strong green color. "Non-living? What non-living?!?"

Edie sighed, a why-must-you-always-question sigh, but she loved it. Her girls were witty and sharp.

She continued. "He, that is God, was the one who designed the ark, so he knew just how big it was going to be. He knew that there simply wasn't room to put all of the animals on the earth into one ship. The ship would have to be monstrously massive."

"Yeah," one put in, "as big as a country!"

"No, it wouldn't. You're being silly."

"Hey, how many animals are on the earth-"

"Girls?" Edie interrupted, bringing their attention back to her. "He considered how he had designed every living thing. He remembered a secret about D.N.A. Well, a secret to us."

Edie squished her finger and thumb together to show a small space between them. "D.N.A. is the tiny particles that make up our bodies. D.N.A. has many pieces that can be combined in thousands, even millions of different ways."

Edie's eyes took on a silver blue tint. "And that's when he developed a plan."

Twin faces nodded. God did make plans.

"God didn't need to put two of every

creature on the ark. He only needed two of every kind of creature. The D.N.A. would do the rest."

"Into the ark God sent two cats, two monkeys, two horses, and so on. When the cats had babies, the kittens would be a different kind of cat, and then the next litter of kittens would be a different kind of cat, and each of those cats would have a different kind of cat, and so on."

"That's impossible," the girls cried.

"Impossible? With God? Yahweh God? No, nothing is impossible with God."

"It's like a musical instrument in an orchestra. What if you only saw and heard the violins and didn't know there were tubas and flutes, trumpets and hand bells?"

Edie smiled the open-hearted smile

that she used when she was teaching them something important.

"You have to remember that God is not only clever and wise, he's sneaky."

The girls grinned. They liked sneaky especially when it involved God and sometimes cookies.

Edie used her toe to lightly push off the porch to set the swing into a lazy drift.

"God could just reach down and touch the mother cat, telling her D.N.A. to play a different set of instruments. Then the kittens would be a different breed of cat. In a few short years there would be all kinds of cats all over the earth again."

"Just think about the dog."

Narrowed, darkly suspicious eyes watched Aunt Edie.

"The dog? Which dog?" The girls' eyebrows crunched into frowns. They were used to Edie's tall tales and were always on the look-out for things that didn't add up.

"Did you know that a dog's cells can be manipulated to make a completely different dog? Think about how some dogs are tiny but look exactly like the regular size one or how a wiener dog is so long but bulldogs are short. What if all animals could change their shape like that?"

Edie shrugged her shoulders. "It's really not that remarkable. Humans mix different breeds of animals all the time. That's how we got race horses. We even do it with plants. I've been working on a new variety of tulip. I'm going to name it Sweets, after my favorite girls."

The girls looked at the garden. Aunt Edie was a master with those tulips. She planted different tulips every season and was always trying to mix them in different ways.

The girls began to imagine. They thought of how parents who have brown hair have kids who were blond. Or how noses can be big on one brother and small on another. Could it be true? Aunt Edie was very smart, but really? Different kinds of cats?

And yet there was the dog.

They pictured every animal and bird and bug that they had ever seen. All the possible combinations of breeds and varieties boggled their minds.

"So, you see," said Aunt Edie, getting up. "That tiny boat was just big enough."

She gave one a kiss on the cheek and the

other a kiss on her forehead then started back to her garden.

The girls looked after their aunt, eyes a fuzzy soft green, wondering, doubtful yet—"Aunt Edie, really?"

Edie paused a moment in thought; her eyes deepened to silver shimmering off the surface of the ocean. "It's either that or spontaneous creation."

Brows leapt with surprise, the girls turned to each other; questions reflected in twin green eyes.

At the flower bed Edie picked up a tulip, her eyes a smiling silver blue.

Aunt Edie, Spontaneous Creation

The twins were spending the night with Edie. These little girls adored staying at their aunt's house but more so trying to catch her in a story.

They were dressed in their pajamas with purple and blue mis-matched socks. In the living room that night, the girls had their heads together, whispering conspiratorially.

"Aunt Edie?" The twins exchanged a look.

Edie paused her knitting needles. She was making scarves for the girls to wear during the holidays. “Yes?”

“You said you would tell us about creating spontinies.”

“Spon-ti-knees?”

“Yeah, Noah’s ark. You said God made the ark just right because he didn’t need all that space.”

Aunt Edie smiled indulgently. The girls thought her smile lit up the sky. “I think you mean spontaneous creation,” she said, setting aside her knitting. She waved the girls over to the couch with her.

“Well,” Aunt Edie began.

The girls grinned at each other. All the best Aunt Edie stories began with ‘Well.’

“You know that God sees and hears all

that inhabits the earth. Even us. Sometimes he watches us for years—sort of like I watch you girls playing in the yard—just delighting in having us near him."

The girls nodded their understanding. They snuggled closer as Edie put an arm around each twin.

"God loves all of the creatures on the earth. He envisions all the animals and birds and bugs that he has ever created and all that he will ever create to walk or fly on the earth."

"He chuckles to himself. God loves to create. He is never closer to the earth than when he is creating. He still creates every day."

The girls sat straight up, elated. "Nope."

Happily, the girls thought they had caught Aunt Edie this time. "He rested on the seventh day," they declared, one confidently gesturing with a finger.

"Oh," said Edie thoughtfully. "I didn't realize that the Bible says that God never created again."

The girls' eyes widened; smiles dropped from their cheeks. The Bible didn't say that.

"I didn't know that creatures can make life all by themselves." Aunt Edie smiled, her face uplifted, as if in thought. A distinct silver began to glow deep in the blue of her eyes.

"We can't make grass grow without God so how could we make a calf or an eaglet, or a baby by ourselves? Remember, only God has the breath of life. Every time there is a new baby, of any kind, God gives it life. Even baby trees receive God's touch."

Gently deflating, the twins settled against her again but continued to listen carefully.

"God loves to surprise us; and he is sneaky." Edie stated.

The girls cautiously nodded their agreement.

"Do you ever wonder if God puts new creatures on the earth when we aren't looking? I've often imagined he does it just for fun."

"That's what she meant!" whispered one sister. "That's why the ark was so small! He could just make them again!"

Edie continued. "People are not always healthy for the earth. Often we do things that harm the animals and birds and bugs."

"That sure is true," said one, shaking her head in disapproval.

"Tsk. Tsk," replied the other. "We've got to do better."

"Sometimes a scientist will search the world over looking for a particular animal that nobody can find."

Edie mimicked a deep voice, "'What's going on here?' God says. 'This isn't supposed to happen for another thousand years.'"

She looked deep into their eyes, "God remembers that animal." She sighed in a gush as her eyes deepened to an ocean blue. "Then he has a decision to make."

"You see, everything on the earth is balanced in intricate ways."

"For every animal there is a counter animal. For every predator, a different predator keeps things in balance."

The girls were transfixed imagining the hierarchy of nature. In their minds, a balance scale system appeared, towering like a tree -similar to ornaments on a Christmas tree. It showed various animals dangling from branches. In some, the tree branch's counter weight pulled downward as others gently rocked in place.

"If a particular bird stops being on the earth, then the opposite bird will cause the weights to get out of balance. If that happens then things could start to spiral."

Spiral?? Green eyes glowed with concern.
"Do they get dizzy?"
"Does it hurt their heads?"
"They would bump into each other."
"Yeah, that could cause—"

Aunt Edie hugged them close. "God sees our failings. And sometimes, sometimes he has mercy on us."

"Where are these animals?"
"Can we visit them?"
"But how does he know which animal is gone?"
"How many of each are there supposed to be?"

Edie paused a moment then shrugged, "I expect he checks his list."

The little girls' eyes narrowed to a sharp green.

What was that?
"List?"
"What list?"

Edie resumed her story. "God picks up a handful of dirt, plucks a few leaves and flower petals for color, scoops up a spray of ocean wave, and begins to form a new creature."

"God is a brilliant maker." Edie's voice warmed to her subject. "He shapes and sculpts the clay until it is a perfect specimen of that creature."

The sisters exchanged a look. "There's that clay again."

"He admires his work. 'Oh, yes,' he says to himself, 'this was a beautiful creation.' He looks down at the earth and decides where to put that creature."

"Sometimes he puts it in a place that scientists don't expect. It's deliberate, I believe. Maybe if we think it's gone, we'll respect it more." Edie nodded for emphasis.

"Then with a gentle wind he leans toward the earth and breathes life into it. And presto, in a few years the earth is in balance again."

Twin chins lifted with suspicion.

"Presto?! Aunt Edie is this true?"
"Can you prove it?"
"Did God tell you that?"
"Where's this supposed list?"
"There is no list in the Bible."

They stared at her with glittering green eyes. This had to be a tall tale but Aunt Edie knew everything and she really loved God. The girls weren't sure what to believe.

She had been right before.

Edie gazed into space for a long moment, "Well, of course, you know that Adam was the first librarian."

Edie smiled as twin faces bloomed to full astonishment, helpless to refute, and yet on the verge of believing.

Aunt Edie, First Librarian

"Librarians were not invented until AFTER books," the twins declared coming into the kitchen.

It was their opening salvo. This time they were determined to prove that Aunt Edie's story was made up.

One of the sisters casually dropped her Bible on the table. They had come prepared.

"What's this," Edie asked. "A challenge to historical detail? I'm glad you are investigating for yourself. Never believe anyone but God."

"We've caught you Aunt Edie. You've made the grand mistake!" one happily declared, certain that triumph was theirs.

"I do like to think of myself as grand," Edie agreed. "I'm a grand baker, a grand knitter—"

"Hey, no diverting."
"You made it up."
"Admit it."

"Did I?" Edie sweetly smiled at her clever, darling girls.

"Uh oh, there's that smile," one whispered.

"No! We can't be wrong. She made it up." Her sister whispered desperately.

"Let me just stir the beans and then we'll talk about God and Adam." Edie said.

A swirl of doubt began a lazy drift through the girls.

Once they were settled on the porch swing, Bible tucked at one's side, the girls rapt, ever watchful for something they could prove, Aunt Edie began her tale.

"So, first God made light."

"Yep, 'Let there be light,'" one of the girls said, nodding confidently.

"Then God made the earth and oceans."

"O.K." Ticking her fingers, the other girl agreed. "Dirt and water."

"Next," Edie paused, "came creepy crawling things that I prefer never to meet."

"She's right. Bugs are gross."

"Yeah, an ant crawled on my leg—"

Aunt Edie cleared her throat. "And there were animals."

"Wait a minute, you forgot the stars. You see," she turned to her sister. "She just says whatever—"

"Yes," Edie smiled indulgently, "God did make the heavens. I thought you wanted to hear about Adam."

"We do."

"Keep going."

"Skip to the Adam part."

"Yeah, tale us the rest," her sister said with a flourish at her joke.

Hiding a grin, Edie continued. "God made lots of animals. There were bugs, and not just the ones we see in the yard. There were birds that covered the skies. And in the deep, in the deep are creatures that we can't yet imagine."

She paused gathering her thoughts; a silvery light began to glimmer in her ocean eyes. "Well."

The girls exchanged looks. "Here it comes, the whopper."

"It always starts with, 'Well.'"

Edie looked at the two most beautiful gifts God had given her.

"Well certainly, there is one human who has seen them all. It was part of the job. Though, I do wonder sometimes if it included drawings."

"You're diverging again."

"What are you talking about?"

"Drawings?"

"There are no pictures in the Bible," they pointed out.

"God is a busy guy. He had other projects to work on."

"Projects? What projects?" Strong green eyes sought her face for any slight of deception.

"Did you think that the earth is God's only responsibility? What about Pluto?"

"Pluto?" Suddenly uncertain, the girls looked at each other. There were other planets. Maybe Aunt Edie had a point. And the stars. Didn't God take care of the stars, too?

"Hmm," Edie continued. "So, he needed someone to finish up."

Twin heads whipped back to watch their aunt closely, faces firmly set.

"Finish?"

"Up?"

Edie nodded, glad that they were

following along. "Yes, the animals needed names."

"Oh no," one groaned.

This couldn't be, the other thought.

"So, God made a man to name the creatures. And why would they need names if God wasn't going to keep track?" Edie shook her head. "God doesn't waste energy like that."

"No," Edie continued. "Adam had a job—"

"But, but—" sputtered one girl.

"Adam was a farmer," said the other.

Edie nodded, "Before he was a farmer Adam's job was to name the animals for God."

She turned from niece to niece, hair swishing. "And no one can keep up with that many creatures without a list. A catalog, if you will."

"A catalog," one said matter-of-factly; twin eyes glaring a deep fathomless green.

"Yes," Edie nodded. "Height, weight, colors, special features, and names. That was the main job, the title of each one; a record of every animal."

"Adam couldn't carry around that many records in a notebook. No," she said, "he needed a record keeping system. A catalog."

Their eyes smoldering with suspicion, the girls stared at each other and then at their beloved, beautiful, sneaky Aunt Edie.

"People who catalog and keep track of something are called librarians."

"Really." The girls' said in unison, their tone was one of challenge.

Edie's smile held secrets of old.

"Of course. How else could God have been sure that Noah had two of every kind?"

Edie shrugged her shoulders, "Or that they would all fit in the ark?"

The girls huffed with frustration and chagrin at being bested again.

Next time. *They would get her the next time.*

Edie hugged her girls, eyes smiling a brilliant silver dancing in the waves of ocean blue.

Chandler

The Halloween Prayer

Halloween was here! The holiest of day of the year. Libby was delighted. She had been practicing The Lord's Prayer all week.

Libby eagerly arrived at the church's fall festival. She beamed as she saw kids and adults running here and there dressed up in all sorts of fun costumes; monsters, ghosts, princesses, and super-heroes.

Libby herself was dressed in royal blue robes for a Statue of Liberty costume. A gray, plush cloth tablet was sewn onto the front of the right side of the robe, beginning just below the waist and stretching almost to the top of her knee. It was unfurling like a rolled up scroll. If one looked closely, they could see bits of words that showed the tablet was of the Ten Commandments.

She held a puffy cloth torch with red and yellow flames which, of course, she alternately stuffed in the pocket on the left side of the robe or squished under one arm.

Her crown sat on her head like a hat with no top, like a sun visor. The yellow crown was a Star of David design that sat flat so that the points of the star could be seen when she tilted her head. In the center of the headband, on her forehead, a small brown cross held up the center star. It really was a lovely costume.

She ran to join her friends. There were

small rides, bouncy houses, cotton candy, and games. They had a wonderful time.

Libby watched the kids all around her in costumes of spirits and demons that they no longer had to fear.

Halloween used to be a time of terrible evil. Horrible things were done in rituals and sacrifices. *Not anymore,* she thought.

As it was getting dark, Libby saw some of the booths had oil lamps that flickered softly in the wind. It reminded her that his Word was like a lamp that showed her the way. She looked down at the sandals that matched her costume, wiggling her toes.

Soon, she expected, they would be gathering for the prayer. She figured that they didn't want to rush the neighbors and families who had come for the candy and games. Not all of them were Christians.

That's really what Halloween is all about, she thought, *making the country safe for everyone.* She knew how important our prayers are.

"Libby? Time to go," her parents called.

"Go? We can't go yet." Libby frowned with concern and alarm that she was going to miss it.

"Come on. It's getting late," her parents said as they loaded the car with left over candy and supplies.

"Kids aren't allowed to join in the prayer?" Libby asked. "But I've been waiting all year."

"What prayer, honey?" Her father was halfway inside the car, putting bags of fall festival stuff in the back seat.

"The Prayer of the Hallows," she said,

sadly looking at her shoes. Being little was not fair to a girl's heart.

Nearby, a long-time family friend was also packing some things into her car. At Libby's words she pulled up short.

"The what?" came a muffled reply from her father. Busy with decorations, he was listening only with half an ear. He reached deep into the car with a scarecrow.

"I want to hallow our country, too. Can't we stay until then?" Today of all days her prayers would not join the others of her community. A small tear formed in her soul.

"Hallow?" The woman asked.

"Hallowed be thy name," Libby quoted, chin lifted with determination, completely confident in her logic. "Today is Halloween."

Looking up to heaven the older woman

smiled with loving appreciation to our God then she took Libby's hand. "I think you're right. We are neglecting our duties. Let's gather God's people and hallow our country."

With her parents following, they called everyone around and explained that Halloween was a time for hallowing. Libby climbed onto a fruit crate so that everyone in the crowd could see her.

"Our Father who art in heaven," Libby began her prayer. "Hallowed be thy name. Today we ask that you hallow our land and our people."

All around the little girl, people of all ages, in all manner of costumes, laid down candy and treats, wherever they were, whatever they were doing, Christians bowed their knees, and joined in the Prayer of the Hallowing.

In that moment God, our God, heard the prayers of his people and hallowed our ground.

And in all the land from year-to-year Halloween was no more a day of fear or evil but a day holy unto God.

A day of hallowing.

The Twelfth Song

It was twelve o'clock when Renée went to lunch one day. She was weary from life's troubles and found that she couldn't sit down to eat; instead, she would spend this time with God. She began to walk.

With her heart so full of sorrow, she could not pray specific words. A few steps went by before her soul spoke directly to God. A song from her childhood began as a whisper.

In a few minutes she was feeling better.

She sang louder. And she felt better. As she walked the parking lot, she sang praises to Jehovah and her spirit lifted higher.

Renée worked right in the middle of town. All around her were small shops and businesses. As cars passed by, neighbors and countrymen went about their daily business, but when the traffic was light her song would float across the street.

Some paused as their ears caught bits of song carried on the wind. A woman putting groceries in her car smiled fondly as she recognized a few words. A man returning the gas handle to the pump nodded along for a few bars. One man of particular kindness was so taken with the song that he sat in his car and quietly sang with her.

Every day the next week during her lunch hour Renée sang to God. She brought sheet music to sing the words to all of the verses.

It rarely seemed to her that she was singing particularly loudly but others did hear and their hearts were lifted.

Of course, Renée could not know, so absorbed in her time with God, that the kind man returned to the parking lot across the street several days that week just to sing along with the walking Christian.

An elderly couple parked their car on a side street with intentions of an afternoon stroll. When they heard her song, they chuckled at first but as they left their car, they picked up the words of her hymn and they too began to sing. They walked all around downtown singing.

Before long the whole town was talking about Renée singing during the twelfth hour. A lifelong Christian, who was mostly house-bound, heard about it from her neighbor who worked downtown. She immediately begged him to go outside during the lunch hour and call her on his phone so that she could sing in time and step.

One day a woman from a nearby business was leaving her office just as Renée was passing by. With a grin the woman matched pace with Renée for a few minutes and joined in the song.

When the kind gentleman found that he couldn't stay shut up in his car any longer, he began walking the parking lot across the street singing along. The next week he picked up a couple of friends on his way downtown and they too just had to sing.

Every day more people from the town joined in with Renée. Without speaking or conversation, with boldness and joy, they sang praises to God. Some were at home, some in their offices; wherever they were at the twelfth hour of the day they sang for love of the Lord our God.

A few weeks later the song was spreading. Folks from the next town began singing songs during the twelfth hour. A young woman mentioned it while chatting with her grandfather who lived across the country.

"Twelve o'clock, you say? She does this every day?" As he hung up the phone his spirit swelled with hope in a way that it hadn't in years. The elderly man wondered if he could do something similar in his town. The next day, standing on Main Street under the tower clock as it struck twelve, he boldly lifted his voice in song and praise. And so spread the song.

A family who went on vacation to another country kept their habit of singing during the twelfth hour. At first the locals thought this funny until they recognized the melody of the music. With a burst of laughter, they joined in. Two languages singing the same song to God. And so, the song flowed to Christians in other countries and to other continents.

Soon in all the world in the twelfth hour the people of God lifted voices to his name in a rolling song of praise and worship. As one time zone ended the twelfth hour, the next time zone began its twelfth hour.

From twelfth to twelfth the song was passed from Christian to Christian, from country to country. In this way the lifting of souls and voices in praise traveled all around the earth.

And in the heavens the Lord of the Heavenly Host heard the song of the souls of his people. The sounds filled his heart with joy.

It pleased him to hear our praises and all around the earth God, our God, blessed his people.

The Dixies

Decoration Day

Today is Decoration Day

We are going to decorate the cemetery.

A cemetery is where we bury the bodies of people who have died. Their souls aren't there, of course, but it's fun to imagine them sitting on the headstones watching the sunset in this beautiful place.

Sometimes I pretend that grandma is sitting on that bench over there sipping iced tea, thinking of the times we played together.

There's a caretaker for the cemetery but he can't do everything. Just keeping the grass cut is a full-time job.

So, one day a year we all come together to get things back in shape.

My first job is picking up the trash. It's terrible what some people will leave lying around.

While I do that, Uncle Nick is climbing trees and trimming branches. Weak limbs can cause problems during a storm. They've got to be cut to keep the tree healthy and growing strong.

Cousin Em is a wiz with the hedge clippers. Shrubs need a good trim just like we need a haircut.

Next, we tackle the worst vine to ever grow in the South. Kudzu. Just saying its name makes us shudder.

The work is so hard that it requires a whistle, as Uncle Nick likes to say. Soon he is whistling his favorite song. It's about a banjo named Dixie. Sometimes some of the older folks will sing along with him. I think they make up the words.

Next, we clean out around the markers. Headstones are big blocks of rock that say who's buried in the grave. I like reading the names of my ancestors, some are really funny.

Finally, we plant new flowers, put fresh paint on the fence, take the trash to the curb. The day is almost over by the time we are finished. Whew! What a job.

I used to think that Decoration Day should be called Work Day but now I know better. Coming here is not about fences and vines. It's all about family.

When the work is done, we spread out

quilts and open coolers full of tea and sandwiches. Then we sit around hearing about everyone's year. I get to tell how I am growing tomatoes in my garden; they taste so sweet. Grandma taught me how to plant tomatoes. I miss her so.

Later we watch June bugs and fireflies light up the cemetery while the older folks tell stories about the people who are buried here. I imagine what life must have been like way back then.

I look around the cemetery. Family members who died before me, those I have known and loved, and we who decorate the cemetery.

Sitting here I realize that we are all together, if only for a few moments. Just for today we are all in the same place.

Flag Day

It all started when I was researching our family tree. I was supposed to draw a tree branch for each family member then list their children but the paper wasn't wide enough.

Great-grandpa and grandma had a lot of kids and they had kids so I had to add more paper. Then more.

Soon the paper was so long that I was worried it wouldn't hold up during my presentation. Mom suggested that I pin the papers to a strip of cloth. We went to the fabric store and found some old sepia cotton.

Instead of pinning the paper tree onto the fabric I drew the family tree right on the cloth using a burgundy brown marker. When I was finished it looked like a faded old newspaper.

Since the cloth was so much bigger, I had plenty of room to pin pictures under some of the names.

The fabric was wider than it was tall so I called it my family flag. My family tree was one of the best in the class.

When I took the flag to our family picnic to show everybody, they all loved it. Now I bring the flag every year. We add new family members for those who were born or got married and put in new pictures.

I loved doing the flag so much that I challenged my cousins to do one of their own. We already had a family tree so we thought and thought what we could do.

We discussed it the rest of the day, tossing ideas back and forth. That was fun, coming up with ways of illustrating our family.

Then Greens and Grady got involved and things got silly for a while. Finally, we decided that each could do their own thing. Whatever they wanted to bring would be fine. It might even be a work of art.

It has become kind of like a scrapbook for our year or a message about ourselves. On my flag for last year I sewed on concert tickets, pictures of my vacation, I drew a masterpiece, and I told a funny story about my grandparents.

My cousin loves quilts so she made her flag with patches of cloth from clothes she outgrew then, she wrote or drew on each square. She even made some of the pieces in the shape of her vacation. I love that beach scene!

Now everyone brings a flag. Of course, they are all in different shapes and styles.

Townsen loves planes. She says she's going to be a pilot or an air traffic controller. Her flag always shows her in some sort of flying machine, most of which probably couldn't actually fly.

Tidwell tries to cram as much on her flag as she can so it ends up being a big mish-mash of every thing she thought was interesting that year. I think she's going to be a designer when she grows up.

Even the adults get in on the fun. Mullvie made a heart then drew cartoon caricatures of her and her new husband. She sewed on a piece of her wedding veil. It was beautiful. Then she pasted on pictures of her new house. She looks so happy. I think they are really in love.

Greens, that's his nickname because he

eats so many collard greens, surprises us each year with some crazy design of old junk he scrapes up around the house. He uses nuts and bolts to make shapes such as people or cars or trees. He tells a story with metal scraps. He's the coolest person I know.

Grady is a gifted artist so he paints a picture each year. He sometimes hides a secret in the design. We have to look real close to see what it is.

This year my flag is made up of letters glued onto canvas. The letters are different styles and sizes. It has small bulletin-sign letters, faded and scratched game tiles, plastic magnet letters and the like.

Grady said it will look art nouveau. I don't know what that means but I hope it means amazing.

I searched everywhere for different types of letters. We spent an entire weekend going to every junk shop, thrift market, and garage sale for a hundred miles around. I didn't quite have enough tiles to finish it so I had to use magazine cut-outs for a couple of letters.

No matter, it sure was fun going to all those second-hand stores. Uncle Greens loves touring the countryside, as he calls it. We had the best time doin' that together.

The letters spell out a poem. It tells about all of my family events this year. You know picnics, holiday dinners, and birthday wishes.

I tried to make the story rhyme but that's harder than it looks. They'll still love it. Just you wait and see.

These days our family picnic is called Flag Day and it's all because of my family tree.

The Gumshoes

The Floating Light

It was a great time to watch the stars. The night sky was clear and the air warm. Lakeland, Travis, and Gage hiked up the hill looking for a perfect vantage point. Something in the distance caught their eye.

A light was floating in the sky. It was a soft glowing yellow. A perfect oval shape.

As soon as she saw it, Lakeland dropped to her knees. Watching the thing in the air, she motioned the boys to do the same.

Travis saw it but, as usual, Gage was more interested in the ground than the sky. Travis grabbed his shirt tail and jerked him down behind some bushes.

Lakeland couldn't believe their luck. They hadn't expected to find anything so soon.

The light floated gently toward the mountains just in front of them.

"What do you think it is?" Lakeland asked. A soft breeze ruffled her hair.

"It's got to be them." Travis said. He was certain that they had found the real thing.

"Gage," Lakeland ordered, "go over to those trees and see how wide it is. Travis, you go down into the valley and see how long it is. Now be careful. We must have exact measurements." Lakeland began rummaging in her bag.

"What are you going to do?" Travis demanded, not entirely sure he liked being ordered around.

Lakeland was impatient at his tone. "I," she explained slowly so he couldn't miss a word, "am going to get pictures of it." She continued rummaging through her bag. "I just have to find my camera."

When her hand closed around the case, Lakeland yanked out her camera. She looked through the view finder and began snapping pictures.

The boys ran to their positions and tried their best to make an estimation of the size of the thing. They hurried back to Lakeland, still hunkered down in the bushes.

"It didn't seem very wide, maybe the size of two trucks next to each other." Gage said, crouching on the ground.

"I think," Travis gasped out, too excited to talk calmly. "I think it's as long as a house."

Lakeland positively glowed with excitement. "A house? Really," she said in wonder.

Travis frowned, "Yes, really. Don't you think that I know how to—"

Lakeland waved him off. "It's coming. Now, look alive boys. Do you hear anything?"

The boys listened.

"No."

"Nothing."

Lakeland watched the light float a little closer.

"Well, they wouldn't need sound."

Travis concluded. "Their crafts defy gravity so they don't need motors and rotors and such, like planes do."

"Right," agreed Lakeland.

"I hear something now," Gage whispered. He didn't want the mysterious light to hear him. It was getting closer.

Lakeland's head whipped around to look at Gage. "What?" She demanded.

Gage cocked his head a moment, listening. "A whisping sound."

"Whisping?" Lakeland couldn't believe her ears. Gage was just making up words.

"Wait a minute," Travis said. "I hear it, too. Kind of a whirring, hissing sound. Real soft like." He scrambled in his pocket to take out his tape recorder. He'd better get this noise on tape. The more evidence the better.

The three children watched the—almost silent—light floating above them. It turned.

The kids gasped. Had it seen them? Should they try to run?

Lakeland saw something that she just couldn't believe. She could barely speak her throat was so tight. "There are shapes. I see symbols," she croaked.

"I see them too!" cried Gage.

"Shush!!" While Lakeland tried to hold her hand steady so that she could take a clear picture, Gage squinted at the shapes.

"Circles. I see a circle. Two circles, I think," he said.

"Yep, I see OO and," – Travis did a double take. "Is that a G?"

"Letters." Travis' voice was filled with

wonder. He pulled himself together and got back to work. "O-O-G?"

"Do you think The OOG are invading!?" Gage's voice shook.

"I don't know," Travis whispered, his head down busily scribbling notes. "Keep watching." He was so excited he wasn't sure that he would be able to read his handwriting tomorrow.

"No," Lakeland said impatiently. "The G is in front. Goo—I can't read the rest. My eyes are blurry. Are those red stripes?"

A stiff breeze blew their hair giving the kids a chill in the warm summer night. The light turned away from them. Now it seemed to be moving sideways.

"Do you think they're searching for something?" Travis asked.

"I can't imagine what. They couldn't know about us already."

"SHO!" Gage cried with delight. "GOOSHO!"

"Shhh." Lakeland chastised. "We have to be quiet or they'll know we're here. Then we might as well give ourselves up."

"Not me!" Travis protested. "I'm not giving myself up to nobody. You just try and make me." He set his chin and gave her his fiercest glare.

Gage was amazed by the light. It was blocking the stars as it floated across the sky. "Look, there are more letters. R—I think that one is a Y. How come they know about the alphabet? When did they learn to read?"

Travis shrugged. "They must've been watching us for years, I guess. There's an

A—hmm, maybe that's another R? Do you see it?" He squinted into the darkness.

Lakeland gasped. She began to shake. "I—I can see them. Inside there. Two beings inside the light."

Gage was stunned. How could this be? Why wasn't the Air Force already out here? How could they just let this thing take over the city; the land; our country?! Someone had to do something.

A gust of wind blew them hard, the light swung toward them. Lakeland squealed in surprise.

Another strong gust blew dirt across their faces, getting in their eyes. When they rubbed the grit away the thing was almost on top of them.

This might be the end. Surely the creatures could see them now. Their parents wouldn't even know what had happened to them. No one would ever know.

"Wait a minute." Gage said. "GOOD – I see the word good. Why would they mark the space ship with English letters?"

Eyes wide, mesmerized by the object, Travis replied, "Maybe it's not English. Maybe those symbols mean something else in their language."

Gage gave him a look. Yeesh, some people would believe anything.

As Lakeland watched the thing, just for a moment she thought she had seen it before. Maybe in a dream?

"Does that look familiar to either of you?" She asked.

"Familiar?" Travis snorted. "Of course it looks familiar. It's a flying saucer, for crying out loud. They all look the same."

"SHOT PHOTOG—I can't read the rest," Gage whispered.

That's when it hit her. Lakeland remembered where she had seen this stripe pattern before.

"Oh no," she groaned.

The wind gusted again. The thing swung wildly for a moment. The beings inside moved to one side.

"Lakeland?" Travis called in alarm. "Are you alright? What have they done to you!"

"Nothing. They've done nothing. Except maybe take our picture."

"Our picture? Naw, they're probably doing brain scans, body scans surely, but not pictures. No, they have our D.N.A. now, so they can just reproduce us at will. They don't need –"

"GOOD SHOT PHOTOGRAPHY!" Gage grinned. He got one. He, Gage Hartigan, had figured out what neither of his companions could. Wow, what a feeling.

He frowned – Photography?

"GOOD SHOT PHOTOGRAPHY—" Lakeland said in disgust, sitting up.

"Hey, get down," Travis cried.

"—is an advertising agency," she continued, putting the lens cap on her camera.

"What?!" Travis sputtered.

Gage frowned looking from the floating light to his good friend Lakeland.

"They specialize in aerial shots. You know, from the air."

"I know what aerial means," protested Gage.

"What are you saying?" Travis demanded.

The light was just above them now. It made a soft whooshing noise as helium gas was shot high up into the balloon.

"It," Lakeland ground her teeth, too embarrassed to talk, "is a blimp. They go up in the sky and take pictures of your house, or the mountains, or a town event."

"A blimp?" Travis queried confused. He looked up at the thing.

"A giant balloon." Gage said softly. He flipped over onto his back so that he could look straight up at the blimp.

The three children watched in wonder as the magnificent, giant balloon floated right over their heads and on through the valley.

They lay there staring up into the night sky for hours later. The stars went on forever.

"I really thought," Lakeland said, breaking the silence.

"Me, too," Travis whispered.

"Well, I guess we did see something extraordinary." Gage said.

They got up, trudging toward their camp.

Lakeland let out a little giggle. "It was kind of funny." She giggled again.

Gage chuckled. "Did you see your face?"

Travis suddenly saw the humor in the whole night. He burst out laughing. "I hope nobody saw us."

The crackle of a twig told them Travis'

dad was coming up the path. “Mornin’ kids. You’re up early. What’cha been doing?”

The kids thought for a moment.

“Aw, just watching the stars.”

“Can’t see the sky from the city like you can out here.”

“Sure am hungry. What’s for breakfast?”

The kids started to follow Travis’ dad back to the campground but for a moment, just a moment they looked up at the sky, the stars winking away in the morning light, and imagined, just imagined what might be.

Cousins, Too

Pearl & Pepper Plan Their Year

The 2nd cousins were in Pepper's bedroom. She was idly sketching Christmas stockings on a scrap of paper.

"Christmas was good but I need a break. A regular schedule." Pearl said, lying on the corner of the bed, straight black hair spilling across the quilt, her sock feet propped up against the wall. With piercing gray eyes, she looked up at a calendar on the wall, upside down, to see what events and plans were coming up. "New Year's Eve is three days away."

Outside the window still-blinking Christmas lights glowed in the trees and bushes.

Pepper smiled. "New events. Fresh days. Each season is a blank canvas in which to paint our hopes and to plan new experiences."

"So formal," Pearl made a face.

With a twinkle in Pepper's storm-cloud gray eyes she turned toward her cousin; her curly black hair bouncing across her cheek. "Are you up for a project?"

Pearl whipped around. "Always. What have you got?"

"We haven't planned out the new year." Pepper was brimming with excitement. "We need to decide on vacations, camps, festivals, do we want to be in a play, so much to choose."

"Let's do it." They ran to get their binders, supplies, and fresh new calendars for the new year.

Pearl and Pepper loved planning things out in advance. That way they could make sure that they got to do absolutely everything.

Pepper carefully laid out her felt tip pens. She used a different color for different parts of her life. School stuff was in blue, family events got orange, special events were always in celebration-red, then for personal events like going to the movies with her cousin she used green, less fun things like doctor visits were always written in black. Even in her calendar, Pepper was an artist.

Pearl didn't care much for different colors of pens. Too much clutter. One clean, easy-to-read blue pen was just fine for her. Opening her new calendar, she admired the rows of neat squares spread out before her.

"First," Pepper pulled out a list. "We need to mark all of the family birthdays and anniversaries."

Quickly they flipped from month to month jotting the name of the person and their event in the square for that date. Pearl's writing was neat and crisp while Pepper's had a bit of flourish. Both girls liked to abbreviate birthday as B.D. and anniversary as Ann.

Pearl noticed Pepper's calendar. "You don't put how old they'll be?"

"No, I just need to know when it is."

"I like to know how old they are. It helps me keep up with their life experiences."

Pearl said with a thoughtful nod at her calendar.

Pepper dug around in her desk drawers until she found the list of major events happening in town. A local ladies group put the list together each year and sold it as a fundraiser for their functions.

"Wait," she paused. "We better go ahead and mark school days since we can't skip those."

With a sigh, Pearl located their school calendar. Of course, the first square the girls marked was the last day of school; stars and squiggly exclamation points for Pepper, bold underlining for Pearl. They wrote in end-of-terms, no-school days, and holidays.

"I do enjoy school but right now the school year looks so long. Summer will never get here." Pepper said with dismay.

"We just have to take it one day at a time," Pearl reminded her. "We'll get through it just like we always do." Eagerly she pulled the community events list toward her. "What have we got this year, ladies?"

They pored over the list together.

"There is the annual pie festival, music and arts festival, city ball games…" Her voice trailed off as she became absorbed in reading the event descriptions.

"We always go to the art festival in April," Pearl mused. "Let me flip back to March to make a note to buy tickets and get a schedule of displays and events. I hope we get some new ideas for craft projects."

For now, the girls wrote down the events they expected to attend. For less important events they made a brief note in the margin of the page for that month.

"The music festival can be fun but I want to wait to see who the main acts will be before making a final decision. We are already rather busy in June." Pepper said, making a note of the dates in the margin of June using red ink with two dollar signs.

With a concerned frown Pepper flipped through the summer months. "Hmm, we are planning a lot of stuff. We're going to have to watch our budget. Have you started one yet?"

"Kind of, I'm jotting an approximate amount next to the event name. I'd better start a cost list month by month." Pearl grabbed a sheet of paper.

"Looks like the museum is going to have several excellent exhibits this year." Pearl commented, her warm gray eyes sparkling with anticipation. "We have to go see the quilt show and, ooh, there is going to be a special speaker on textiles and dressmaking with a week-long display of the history of needlecrafts."

They each made a note to renew their annual pass, busily scribbling dates and notes in the little squares of their calendar days.

Next the cousins consulted an online ticket website to find out which concerts would be coming to town. Pepper was excited to see that their favorite Christian band was coming in September. That, too, was written into a square as Pearl added it to the budget, five dollar signs.

"What are they doing at the theater this year? Do you want to perform in one of the plays? Maybe help with the sets and costumes?" They pulled up the website for the local theater. They loved going to plays. The cousins browsed the shows that the theatre group would perform in the next play season.

"They've got some good shows but I don't want to be in either of them. How about you?"

"Naw, I've got too many other things going on to manage rehearsals and performances. Let's try to attend this comedy and I love a ghost story." Pearl tapped the schedule sheet with her pen. "If we go to the Thursday show we can get a discount and help our budget."

Pepper looked at her notes of the things she wanted to do this year. "I was thinking of planting a vegetable garden this year but it was so hard to take care of last time we tried it."

"This year I'm prepared." Pearl stated. She pulled a book from her tote bag. "I bought an almanac for gardeners. It'll tell us when the ground has warmed enough from the winter cold and it recommends times for planting different plants, flowers, and vegetables. We'll do better this time."

Just reading the different entries in the almanac was overwhelming. Pepper wasn't sure that she could manage all this stuff. "When will we find time to weed and water and plant and –"

"We'll manage." Pearl replied with a wave of her hand. "What movies are coming this year?" She rummaged around until she found the magazine page she'd saved that listed the major movies coming soon. The girls eagerly pored over the descriptions of movies they thought they would like to see.

She picked up her pen to mark the release of an adventure. "Wow. The year is filling up already." Pearl flipped to the summer months. She had a long list of places she wanted to go. They hadn't even thought of the biggest summer event of all.

Vacation is a serious matter, not to be taken lightly, Pearl thought. "Have the folks said anything about vacations yet?"

"My dad said we can pick some short trips if we want to but don't forget about church camp. We'll be gone four days for it," Pepper replied.

"When is the knitting workshop we want to attend? I don't want to miss that. My grandmother might go with us."

After a quick consultation of the flier, they had on both, they each marked those in the appropriate months.

"Now, down to the business of vacations!" They checked the tourism websites for all of the places they would like to visit. "Let's get a guide for the city. Mom said she has airline points that we can use. And we'll want to go to the beach for a few days. How about that storytelling festival? Should we get a county guide this year?"

Her cousin nodded. They immediately requested a vacation guide for all the places that had tempting events or shows that were in easy driving distance and plenty that weren't.

"Our parents aren't going to let us take all of these trips."

"Hey, we can hope," Pearl protested, "and when necessary, wheedle extra trips."

The guides had descriptions and pictures of all kinds of things a city or state had to offer. Just from the websites the girls found several sights they wanted to see. This was so exciting the cousins couldn't wait to get the brochures and finalize their plans.

"When should we go?" Pepper squealed. "There's so much to do!"

Together they pored over the couple of months in the summer when their families could get away.

Pearl reviewed her calendar. "June is rather booked. What, with the music festival and a play. There are several birthday dinners but we could pinch in a few days between church camp and the 4th of July. That would free up the next week for the craft workshop that we want. It runs three full days. If we book now—"

"Hey," Pepper groused. "I don't want to rush through our vacation then go straight to something else. I need time to breathe, you know. After vacation I'm going to try out all the new stuff I saw. Art things!"

Pearl tried to keep her cool. *No need to fuss. There was time enough for everyone.*

Looking over her calendar, she had to agree with her 2nd cousin. "I really do want to spend a few days just reading books."

"My grandparents are going on a cruise so I have to save time for when they'll be here to do things with them. This summer I was hoping to learn some new painting techniques." Pepper looked at her calendar with a worried frown.

"Well, there you go." Pearl said, moving on. "We'll use that time to do this other stuff. This is the week that the new action adventure opens. We'll go to that Friday."

"There is a double header at the ball park that weekend. My favorite player will be there. We have to do that." Pepper put in. "Make sure the budget allows for a souvenir. I want to get a signed shirt. And I want the double toppings hot dog special."

Pearl flipped to that month in her

calendar. There were multiple events every day that week, the week after had a long arrow through it with "Vacation" written across, and the week before had an arrow with "Camp" written on it.

The image of the calendar grew large in her eyes. So much to do. So many appointments. Suddenly the stress of all these activities began to squeeze Pearl's brain.

"Wait!" She cried gasping a breath. "Wait," she breathed slowly snatching at calm. "This is too much. I can't plan what I am going to eat six months away unless it's absolutely necessary."

Pepper looked at squares of her calendar that were so full that the date numbers were hardly visible. Next to her was a pile of brochures and notes on events that hadn't been touched yet.

She slouched down in her chair. "Maybe," she began carefully, "we are overdoing it. I guess we don't need to plan which movies to see." Her eyes narrowed at the baseball schedule. "But I am going to that ball game."

Now that she could breathe Pearl threw a sidelong glance at her favorite cousin. A grin split her face. Pepper was fierce when defending what she wanted.

Pearl's eyes roamed over the pages of dates and schedules piled around them. "So, maybe we could just mark the things that we each find most important."

"What if we only write in things that are yearly, like birthdays? Then we could just add the biggest events." Pepper too, was trying to compromise.

The girls were concerned. They didn't want to miss anything and the key to that was planning ahead.

With a huffy sigh, Pearl gave in to practicality, "O.K. let's get rid of all the things that we can do any time or any day."

With a thick black marker, they crossed off movies and museum trips.

Reviewing the schedule for the local community events, Pepper speculated, "I guess we could decide on these as they get closer."

They marked through the music festival, the plays, and the art show.

"Camp is essential so we'd better leave that."

"And the concert. The band doesn't come this way every year."

On the girls went discussing the importance and limitations of each of their plans until their year began to be hopeful again.

"Whew, it's a good thing we started early. Who knew this was so hard." Pepper said, flopping onto her bed.

A frown crinkled Pearl's face. Her fresh clean pages of those little perfect squares were now a mess. Her eyes lit up with an idea. "Want to go shopping? I need a new calendar."

Pearl & Pepper Redecorate Their Rooms

A few days into the summer Pearl came home from shopping with her mom. She had grown so much this year that her summer clothes didn't fit anymore.

Once she had tossed the new clothes into the washing machine, she went to her room. There was a big task ahead of her.

New clothes meant the old ones had to be evaluated, sorted, and weeded. Could she still fit into them? Were they too worn to keep?

It was time to clean out her closet.

She pulled out some shorts sets. She knew right away they were too small. One had the cutest kitten print. Another was a princess top with a sparkly crown on the shirt. Pearl grinned to herself. Both were pink, of course.

As she dropped them on the bed a pillow caught her eye. It too was pink. Looking around the room there was a lot of pink.

She used to love pink. She wanted pink curtains, pink bed linens, pink slippers, pink carpet – *thank goodness mom had said no to that*. The whole bedroom was done up in shades of pink and soft white. Now it seemed like there was too much of a good thing. She giggled as she imagined she was living inside a swirl of cotton candy.

Suddenly her room didn't feel as luxurious as it used to. Pearl no longer felt like a princess spinning on top of a music box. The ruffles of pink lace and the crown on a peg above her desk all seemed dinky, even cluttered. Everything in her room looked so girl-ee. Like a little kid.

I must have grown in more than just height, Pearl thought. She picked up the phone and called her cousin.

"I need a new room." She blurted out, surprised at how annoyed she sounded.

A few doors down the street Pepper was painting. Dabbing the brush in blue paint, her storm-cloud gray eyes focused on the canvas, "Another room?"

Trying to catch the shaded-blue of the underside of a cloud, Pepper squinted out the window.

"I just decided," Pearl said firmly. "I don't want to live in this room anymore."

Pepper was surprised. Usually, Pearl was so down-to-earth. "You want your parents to move because you don't like your room anymore?"

"No," Pearl rolled her eyes, flopping onto her bed. She stared up at the pink gauzy canopy. "I don't want a new house. I want a new room."

"Oh," Pepper swiped more light blue paint across the canvas. "What's wrong with it?"

"It looks like I'm in a giant piece of bubble gum. Everything is pink. All we need is some cartoon funny papers for the wrapper and we'd be set."

Pepper imagined Pearl's room. "You're right. I never noticed it before." She thought for a moment. "I think my room is just about the same. All light green. I used to love mint."

Looking around her room with a critical eye, she noted that most items in the room were some shade of minty green.

A small smile began at the corners of her mouth. The more she looked the funnier it was. She began to giggle. "I think I'm a leprechaun," she laughed.

The cousins each surveyed their rooms seeing the old and familiar. In their respective rooms their eyes began to gleam. There was nothing these two girls liked more than a project.

"I don't like pink anymore. I want a change." Pearl said.

"Me to, me to," Pepper said with a grin.

She jumped out of her chair. “I’ll be right over.”

Moments later the girls were ready to start their new project. They each scrambled to flip their notebooks to fresh sheets of paper; Pearl to write a list, Pepper to sketch ideas.

Pearl thought for a second. “I need a new bed. The canopy is too frilly.” Her clear-gray eyes surveyed and assessed each item in the room. “And curtains.”

“We need a whole new theme. Magazines should give us some ideas.” Pepper mused, picturing her own room.

“I’m thinking a new bed gets new linens. I’ve got to have a larger bookcase or stop buying books.” Pearl was turning around the room pointing out each feature.

“My desk is rather small,” she continued.

"When we work on projects, we have to use the bed to lay out materials."

Really getting into the excitement, Pepper's mind filled with ideas. "I want a drafting table. A big one with a light box."

Pearl tapped her pen on her chin. "Of course, I must have new furniture. These dressers are too small."

"We can do everything up in a period. You know an era, like Queen Anne, then—"

"Do you think we could get these windows re-done into a bay window style? Then we can have a window seat—"

Quickly flipping to a fresh page, Pepper's pencil flew across the page. "I could really use new lighting. Some sconces would soften the overall affect and we could get a lighting expert to make sure that it more closely mimics sunlight. Then I could paint and draw even at night. Good lighting is essential—"

Still in her own thoughts, Pearl continued, "You know dear cousin, I have always wanted a swing in my room. Wouldn't it be grand to be able to—"

"A swing? You want to swing in your bedroom? The ceiling would have to be raised at least three feet to be even remotely safe. There is no way that your folks will allow you to raise the roof."

Irritation spiked Pearl. "Not a jungle gym swing. A porch swing. I don't want to soar only rock gently," she took on a dramatic breathy voice that she thought made her sound mature, "into the night."

Pepper burst out laughing. "—into the night? Get a rocker. Cheaper, easier to move, and no roof raising required."

Pearl glared. 2nd cousin or not, her swing was important. "I'm growing up and I want a room to match the new me," she grumbled.

Hiding her face behind the sketch pad, Pepper tried hard to tamp down her giggles, floppy curls bouncing.

With a twist of her mouth and a narrowing of her eye Pearl sat. She took a moment to re-group. "How about we just get some magazines and consider ideas."

"Love it." Pepper replied. In a flash she was up and racing to the recycling bin. She rummaged through the bin until she found several magazines then swiped a couple of brand new ones from the mail pile on the hall table.

A few minutes later with cheese crackers and sweet tea in hand, magazines scattered across the floor, the girls pored over the pages. There were so many choices and possibilities.

They tore out pages that had things they liked; a painting in one, a pile of pillows in another. Pepper sketched ideas as Pearl worked on a budget comparing their savings with the expected costs.

"I don't think we can afford this. We need some furniture. We weren't planning on these expenses." Pearl mumbled to herself.

Pepper began pinning the pieces of paper onto a bulletin board in a kind of collage. When she couldn't pin another cutout to their board Pepper said, "It occurs to me that we may be overdoing it."

With a toss of her pen Pearl's head sank down onto her ledger, silky black hair spilling over the page. "I hate to give up but I have to agree."

"What are we really talking about here? How much do we have to do right now?" Pepper looked around the room mulling over the situation. "Let's try cutting out a few of the bigger and expensive stuff. Later, we can work those in over the next year."

"Sure," Pearl pulled herself up. She flipped to a new page in her notebook. "We have to get rid of the colors. So, new paint. I am getting too tall for the bed."

Pepper nodded her agreement. "Changing the carpet would be too much right now. I guess ultimately new sheets and quilts and maybe some curtains? What do you think?"

"Throw in a couple of artistic touches and I'm all in." Pearl agreed with pleasure.

A few days later the girls had talked their parents into letting them paint their rooms. Best of all, their parents had agreed to buy new beds and toss in a few bucks for other items.

The girls started by clearing out the furniture and putting on a fresh coat of paint. This gave them a perfect excuse to camp out in the backyard.

A quick trip to the store took care of new bed sheets and new lamps for their side tables. The fabric store had plenty of material that would work for curtains—as if they would buy curtains off the rack! Not these cousins. They spent a few hours measuring and sewing.

The last thing they needed was new quilts for their beds. They pulled out every quilt their families owned. It was a hard choice. Each quilt was its own work of art but finally Pepper and Pearl each had a quilt that suited their newer selves.

It took the girls two days to put their new

rooms together. They tried the furniture over here, over there. Should the bed face the window or to one side? Everything had to be arranged and tested several times before they were satisfied.

"The walls are a bit bare." Pepper noted.

"Maybe we could put up some shadow boxes."

"I wonder if we could do some mini-quilts as wall hangings."

"Perhaps just a few paintings and pictures for now?"

"Too bad we don't have an artist in the family." Pearl tossed out with a wiggle of her eyebrows.

They raced to Pepper's art trunk where she kept her finished pieces. Riffling through her recent paintings and sketches, the girls quickly found more than enough to fill their walls. An hour later the cousins left the craft store, arms laden with frames and hooks.

Finally, hanging their clothes into their newly painted closets they could see the results of their efforts. Each room was a perfect fit in character and style. Splendid.

A day or so later the girls were sitting in Pepper's new room. Pearl had a notebook, studying a ledger and her lists. Pepper examined a sketchbook showing fabric swatches and pictures from magazines that were glued to the pages.

"We almost did it." Pearl said. "Just about a week's allowance over budget."

"I can live with that." Pepper said then grabbed at the sketchbook as it slid off of her lap. "Now about that drafting table—"

Pearl & Pepper Make A Cookbook

"We'll use Ossie's cobbler and I'll whip up a couple of my pies. Do you think Chelsie will bring her famous pot roast?" said grandmother Grace.

Pepper and Pearl lounged at the kitchen table while Pepper's mom and grandmother planned a big dinner. The whole family was coming. The cooking would take all day.

On the counter was an open square tin, Pepper could make out a worn logo from a tea bag company. A small flower blossom was next to the faded, scratched image of two ladies in sunhats and sundresses on a porch sipping from glasses of iced tea.

The tin was chock-full of pages that had been torn out of magazines, newspaper clippings, and some plain white pages with scribbled notes and food stains.

Occasionally the two women would briefly consult a weathered recipe from the box. As they planned, her mom made notes on a scrap of paper.

Pepper's grandmother flipped through a battered cookbook that had a bunch of different recipes stuffed in next to the regular pages. "We should call Cody to get the ingredients for his casserole. He can mix it up once he gets here."

Grace continued, "I know she's got a big project at work, but maybe Lori will have time to make her herb and cheese bread." She opened the pantry to check for staples.

Pepper pulled the recipe box toward her. Some of the pieces of paper were just scraps. One recipe was written on a napkin, the ink had seeped all the way through the thin paper. The recipe title was barely legible as '*cheese biscuits*,' then scribbled ingredients.

Meanwhile, Pearl's eyes wandered around the kitchen. Could she sneak a snack? She spied some leftover cornbread wrapped up on the stove top.

"A tomato salad would be nice." Pepper's mother checked for tomatoes.

"I love tomato salad," Pearl said to her cousin as she swiped the cornbread.

"Do you think we can make all this stuff when we get older?" Pepper watched her mother and grandmother conferring over side dishes. "I'm not very good with cooking."

"Don't worry," Pearl was busy unwrapping the wedge of cornbread. "It's just mixing and following the directions."

"Directions?" Pepper's mind spun at the thought of keeping up with all of the ingredients, measurements, and cooking temperatures.

"Yep," Pearl said around a mouthful of cornbread. "The recipe. We'll make copies. It's just like a pattern."

"Mom? Where are the recipes for these dishes?" Pepper asked.

Her mother was distracted. "Recipes? There are a few here in the cookbook." She riffled frozen vegetables in the freezer then made a note on her list.

"Honey, we've made these dishes for

so many years we know them by heart." Grandmother Grace tossed over her shoulder.

Listening to her elder women Pepper realized that most of the foods for family dinners weren't in a cookbook. Were they written down anywhere?

The girls wandered into the living room but Pepper couldn't get her favorite foods off of her mind.

Maybe I can write down some of the recipes at the dinner next week, then I'll have them when I grow up, Pepper thought.

"My mother and grandmother don't have the recipes written down. They make the foods from memory. What if we made up recipe cards for special dishes?" She suggested to her cousin.

Pepper thought about it for a moment.

"We could write the recipes on note cards and put them in a pretty box."

"What a great idea," Pearl said. "I'll do one for me and my mom, too."

They started making notes as they brainstormed how to put together a box of recipes.

"We'll need to get some note cards and write down each recipe five times so that we all can have one," Pearl said.

"Six," Pepper said. "We're going to need six sets. If I don't give one to Aunt Viveau, she won't give me a batch of her fudge for Christmas." She looked at Pearl with meaning. "I need my fudge."

"Wait. Who are you counting? Just us, moms, and grandmas is six. Plus, Viveau is seven. Pepper, we can't make a box for everyone. That would take ages." Pearl said with concern.

Pepper checked her notes. "If we give one to every house," she counted relatives on her fingers, "that would be at least fifteen, well more really." She made a face imagining all the work. "Maybe we need to re-think this. Maybe we should just do one for ourselves."

Pearl thought it over. "It sounds like a lot of work for just us. It would be nice to give a collection of family recipes to each relative."

"Christmas is a couple of months away." Pepper's eyes were pensive as she thought into the future.

Then Pearl noticed a scrapbook they had made last year. Her face lit up.

"What if we made a cooking scrapbook? I mean not a scrapbook exactly. More like a cooking recipe scrapbook." Pearl said. "We could type up the recipes on the computer and print the pages on pretty paper."

Pepper thought about the scrapbook they'd made. "We could add photos of family members or pictures of finished dishes."

"And funny comments as captions." Pearl's eyes filled with the excitement of a new project.

The girls hurried to call every relative they could think of to ask them to send their special recipes.

At the craft store a few days later they considered the possibilities. "O.K." Pearl said. "We need some colored printer paper. What should we use for a cover? Cardboard or maybe soft plastic?"

"Maybe we could cover the cover in

fabric." Pepper scanned the shelves. "I wonder if we should just use a ringed binder."

"I like the idea of a binder for adding new stuff later on but I also really want a finished polished book." Pearl sorted through the supplies.

After much searching and discussion, they chose colored printer paper for the recipes and a cream card stock for the cover then found some heavy-duty book glue.

Back at home the recipes were pouring in. Already a pile of mail was waiting for them. Several were in different sized envelopes that held pictures.

Eagerly, the girls began typing up each recipe, making sure to double check every measurement. Once they were satisfied that the recipes were correct, they printed the pages on plain white paper.

Pepper held up the sheets frowning, "This paper is too big."

"I guess cookbooks are smaller than regular paper." Pearl replied.

Quickly they measured some of the cookbooks from the kitchen. Standard 8x11 paper was too big.

Pearl ran her hands through her hair, glaring at the cookbooks. This project was getting more complicated. "We're going to have to cut the pages down to size."

Sighing at the work ahead of them, Pepper went to get the recipes they'd already typed up. They spent the rest of the day with ruler and pencil mapping out the size the pages would be once they were cut. Pepper marked up the printed recipes while Pearl marked up the pretty paper and cardstock for the covers.

By the end of the week the cousins were ready to sift through photo albums for pictures to match up to each recipe. They piled up at the dining room table with a stack of photo albums, envelopes, and shoeboxes all crammed with photographs.

"Grandma Glory looks so pretty. I forget that she was a young woman once." Pearl smiled fondly.

Pepper burst out laughing. "Look as these clothes!"

They laughed at the funny hairdos from when their relatives were kids. It was a great afternoon. Gradually they found different photos of each person who had given recipes.

"O.K." Pearl always said this when she wanted to gather her thoughts. "We need to match pictures up to the food."

They placed the photos next to the recipes, swapping different pictures around until they liked each page layout.

"We should call this one 'Sweet Kisses Cookies,' Pepper giggled at a photograph of an older relative kissing the top of a baby's head.

They worked out captions to write below each photo. Next, they used a stencil to draw a border around the edge of the pages. Very carefully they used a mildly-sticky putty to fix the pictures to the recipe pages.

"Careful," Pearl warned. "If we damage these pictures, we won't get to eat at family dinners for a long time."

It was getting dark and the moon was rising when they drew the curtains and flipped on lamps.

"I'm getting fuzzy." Pepper rubbed her

forehead, swiping curls off her face. “Let’s lay them side by side. I need to see them all together.”

The cousins laid out six taped and marked up pages side by side across the floor; more pages were stacked up nearby.

“Now we need to scan the pictures into the computer, crop them to size and place them next to the recipes.” Pearl began gathering up the pages then stopped, her eyes lids were drooping. “Tomorrow.”

“How about next year,” grouched her cousin. “Why do we start these things?!”

“There are days and days of work still.”

“How about tomorrow we just box this stuff up.”

“Hide it in a closet.”

“And go to a movie?”

Both girls were tired and out of sorts.

Sweeping the whole project into a box, they went to bed.

A few days later, spirits refreshed, they were back at it. Pearl scanned the photographs on the scanner, while Pepper manned the computer. She adjusted the pictures onto the recipe pages then typed in headings and captions.

Once each page was carefully designed, they printed the pages first on regular paper and checked for mistakes. A few minor adjustments later they were ready to print their books.

"This paper is perfect. Let's do a different color for each recipe." Pepper loaded the printer. As they printed, she placed each recipe in piles on the table. "Use the paper cutter to start cutting off the excess then we'll put the pages in order." She told Pearl.

In a few hours the pages were cut to size,

in order, and neatly stacked. Finally, they were ready to assemble each book. Their eyes gleamed with the excitement.

"I researched how to do the cover." Pepper said. "Fold the card stock around the stack of pages then mark where the pages fit in the center and put a crease on either side. That way it will wrap around the recipes allowing the spine of the book to be flat."

Pearl scooped up a pile of recipes but when she tried to fold the card stock, she lost her grip and the pages took flight. "Aack!" she squealed.

"You have to hold them tight," snapped Pepper.

"You hold them tight. I'll fold," fumed her cousin.

Getting the spine of the covers to crease

around the pages was a little tricky at first but the cousins finally fit the pages neatly in the middle of the card stock.

Pepper admired their results. She loved seeing a project as it developed.

Pearl found a popsicle stick to smear the glue and began gluing the spine edges of the papers to the interior spine of the covers.

They double checked each set of pages to be sure that no edges were sticking out and that the card stock would fit tightly just like a regular book. They took heavy books from their bookshelves and stacked them on top of their creations to press the glue tight until it was dry.

Later that week they were ready for the next step. “They’re dry. I’ll get the stencils and we can write in the title.” Pearl drew a faint line across the middle of each cover and began stenciling in the letters.

"This is too boring. We've put too much work into this thing to just do a title." Pepper said, ever the artist. She stared at the pretty card stock for a minute. In a flash of inspiration, she snapped her fingers. "I've got it. Cartoons!"

"Cartoons?" Pearl objected. "I am not pasting the funny pages to these beautiful books."

Pepper rolled her eyes. "Not the Sunday comics. I'll draw a cartoon of our relatives cooking," she said with a lopsided grin.

Pearl wasn't convinced. Drawing was harder for her so she didn't visualize the finished product so easily. *This was part of the charm of making homemade gifts,* she shrugged, *the challenge and discovery and personal touch.*

Eagerly Pepper picked up her pencils then swiped a large piece of scrap paper.

She did some rough sketches of each relative who would receive a cookbook.

For Uncle Cody, Pepper drew him at a barbeque grill with a ball cap on his head. Her mother was at the table with flour smeared on one cheek as she made cookies. Aunt Ossie, one of the Greats, wore a knitted vest and had her hair in a pony tail as she pulled a cobbler from the oven. Each relative got their own caricature drawing with large heads, smaller bodies, and exaggerated scenes.

"Pepper this is going to take all day." Pearl glared at her cousin's bent head.

"Yeah, but it'll be worth it. I'll do the outlines and features; you color them in."

By the time they had drawn comics for each book the girls were worn out. Over tea and tomato sandwiches they reviewed their work. Proudly Pepper and Pearl admired the collection of family recipes.

With a pretty ribbon tied around each book they were finished. They couldn't wait to give out the cookbooks on Christmas Eve when all of the family would be together.

"Hmm," Pearl surveyed the stacks of books. "How shall we wrap them?"

Pepper's eyes grew wide with the possibilities.

Pearl & Pepper In The City

"Two days in the big city!" Pearl squealed. "A sleep-away field trip."

Cousins Pearl and Pepper perched on the edge of their seats at the dining room table eagerly poring over a brochure about the city.

"I hope we get to walk through the sculpture gardens. Maybe we can get some good pictures."

"The city overlook provides a great view. I want to sketch the skyline."

The girls were excited. Their class was going to the city to visit a museum, see a play, and go to a big league ball game.

Later that night their moms offered to pack for them but they each begged to do it themselves. They were getting older and this was a grown up thing to do.

Full of confidence Pearl grabbed the telephone. "I get to pack all by myself," she said.

"Me too." Pepper responded. They propped the phones up so that they could pack together.

Pearl turned to her closet. "I'm going to take my purple skirt and my new shoes." She tossed those on the bed then turned back to the closet.

Pepper, too, began pulling out clothing.

"Ooh, this shorts set is gorgeous."
"I may go to the gym at the hotel."
"What if I feel like jeans tomorrow?"

And on went both girls, too excited to be practical, usually their lead quality.

In Pepper's room she picked up a large sketch pad and a box of expensive colored pencils. "Hmm, do you think I should put my pencils in a baggie so they won't take up so much room in my suitcase?" She glanced at the pile of clothes already on the bed. "Yeah, that'll make them easier to carry, too."

"I'm taking my new camera," Pearl said, not having noticed Pepper's comments. "It has a long zoom so we can get close up details and there's extra lenses. I can't wait to try it out. There's going to be so much to see."

"Which book are you taking to read once we're in the hotel room at night?" Pepper asked, surveying her overflowing bookshelf. A thick guidebook was already next to the suitcase. It was paperback, of course, as a hardback cover would be bulky to deal with while they walked around town.

"I think a history of the city is appropriate. Don't you?" Pearl tossed onto the bed a large volume that they had bought a few weeks ago.

Before long the girls each had a suitcase bulging with clothes, shoes, and things they couldn't live without for the day-and-a-half trip.

The next day the girls lugged their heavy cases to the big tour bus that would take them into the city. Their teacher smiled at each student as they took a seat. The bus was so high up it was like looking out a second story window.

The first thing that they did when they arrived in the city was to check into the hotel. Pepper and Pearl got to share a room with two huge beds. Their window overlooked the city skyscrapers, grand steepled churches, and gleaming business towers.

The girls felt so mature as they changed clothes to go to dinner and then to a play. Pearl had brought a sweater to wear with her dress but Pepper only had a jean jacket. It would look awful with her elegant pantsuit so she left it in the room.

Dinner was a formal affair with water glasses and soft light. Large vases stood on insets along one wall with tall, bold, elegant flower arrangements of irises and lilies beaming with color. One wall was tall windows showing the city's nightscape.

Pearl blushed with pleasure. "I feel like a real lady. Look at that chandelier."

"We have to do a fancy table design as soon as we get home!" Pepper whispered. She gently tapped their glasses together in a toast.

While waiting for the city bus to take them to the theater the kids marveled at the people of the city. There were so many everywhere. A brisk wind whipped around the skyscrapers.

Pepper shivered. "Who knew it was so cold here?" She wished that she had brought her jacket.

"It's the huge buildings. I read about it last year when I studied city design." Her cousin said with helpful nod. "The buildings are so large and tall that they push the current around them forcing the wind down into the narrow streets causing it to speed up."

In the theater the architecture and décor were spectacular. Pepper whipped out her sketchpad almost as fast as Pearl uncapped her camera. Settling into plush seats, they scanned the program.

"The play is about Dracula."

"Period costumes from the 1800s."

"Look at those velvet stage curtains, floor to ceiling."

"We could add crown molding in our rooms."

"The scroll work around the lighting sconces should be easy to replicate. I'll take a couple of pictures."

During the play two women chatted on stage as a man approached with the air of a hunter. He was dressed in a dark suit with a cape that cascaded over his shoulders. Even with the high drama of the moment, both girls imagined how the cape would look as part of future costumes of their own.

Back at the hotel that night the girls were consumed with the wonder of the big city. Out their window, the lights mapped a grid of each neighborhood and high-rise.

They chatted about the things they had seen until the excitement began to wind down.

"I'm tired." Pepper yawned. "I've got to get ready for bed." She was glad to scoot under the covers. She had been chilly all night. Pearl was just getting into bed when she realized that she didn't have her favorite book.

"Oh no!" she exclaimed.

"What?! What?" Pepper sat up. Had Pearl seen a bug? She looked suspiciously at the floor.

"My Bible. I left it at home on my night table. I can't sleep without my Bible," she all but wailed. She knew that some hotels put a Bible in a drawer but it wouldn't be the same as her own.

"Don't worry, you can share mine." Pepper gently smiled holding up her Bible.

Pearl was so relieved. She and Pepper had the same Bible so it would almost be like hers. She climbed into bed next to Pepper and they read a Bible verse together.

Pearl looked across to the other bed. It seemed so big and so empty without any of their adult relatives.

"We normally sleep in the same bed

when we travel anyway," Pepper said, a lilt of hope in her voice. "Maybe you could—"

"Yes," Pearl said with relief. "I should just stay here with you."

Snuggled together, the girls were soon asleep.

The next morning, they were up early for a visit to a museum. After that they would go to an afternoon ball game.

Pepper raced into the shower. She picked up a little bottle of shampoo from a basket on the counter and poured some into her hand.

"Ugh," she said. "This stuff smells awful. I can't use this. My allergies will be terrible." She leaned out of the shower.

"Pearl," she shouted. "Bring me your shampoo."

Pearl hurried in. “I didn’t bring any. Mom said that the hotel would have shampoo.”

Pepper held out the little bottle. Pearl sniffed, “I can’t use that,” she exclaimed.

In dismay the girls looked at the shampoos and soaps in the basket. The hand soap was unscented so when the girls had washed up the night before they hadn’t noticed the other products were fragranced.

“We’ve got to hurry. For now, we’ll just have to use the hand soap.” Pearl said.

Pepper rubbed the little bar of soap into her curly hair, making a mental note to always bring her own shampoo in the future.

Breakfast was quick then the group headed out to the museum. Pearl had chosen to wear her purple skirt and new shoes.

The museum was magnificent. There was an atrium that rose four stories high to a domed ceiling. There were statues that were so tall the girls had to climb stairs to a platform to see the top. Paintings, ancient instruments, and pottery all amazed and delighted.

The floors were their own work of art. Each square tile created intricate patterns. Pearl took a picture of a few of the designs. Maybe they could do something similar in a craft.

As they moved to a new exhibit Pepper noticed Pearl grimace. "What's wrong?"

"My feet are killing me." Pearl whispered. "I wish I could just take these shoes off and go barefoot."

Scandalized, Pepper looked around to see if anyone had heard. "You can't do that. This is a museum!"

"I know," her cousin said crossly. "Next time I won't bring new shoes. I'll make a note as soon as we get back to the hotel." Turning to follow their classmates she resolutely tried to focus on the exhibits.

In the gift shop they bought a large oversized book of paintings and each picked out a poster of the piece of art that had most impressed them that morning.

The girls left the gift shop lugging a full sack. Arms were soon tired as they each carried their stuff. Pearl hiked the strap of her camera over her shoulder as Pepper dropped several colored pencils while trying to balance her sketch pad under one arm.

Once at the ball park Pearl began to cheer up. She slipped off her shoes to watch the game. Their seats were fantastic but she had forgotten that ballparks have very little shade.

"I need a hat." Pearl turned to Pepper who was watching the progress of the hotdog hawker.

Pepper snatched up her change purse. "I'm starved. Want a hotdog?" She licked her lips. "I want a dog loaded with kraut and mustard," she paused savoring the memory of dogs past, "and maybe some chili."

"Those guys don't have toppings just little packets of ketchup. For toppings we have to go up to the food stands, which, I need a hat anyway." She squashed her feet back into the shoes.

At the kiosk the girls bought hats, t-shirts, and pennants as well as dogs and slushies. To Pearl's delight the vendor also sold flip-flops. She paid a fortune for them but her toes serenaded her with glorious gratitude.

With hats smashed down over their

hair the girls headed back to their seats. Their team t-shirts were thrown over their shoulders while they tried to carry food and drink.

Pearl also had to balance her shoes under one arm. The edge of a pennant was stained with the slushy that she had in the same hand. Pepper, of course, already had a smear of mustard and chili at the edge of her mouth and tip of her nose where she had taken a bite of her hotdog.

Trying to squeeze past the other fans in the seats without dropping anything was more than Pearl could manage. Her shoes fell on the woman in front of her.

"I'm so sorry," sputtered Pearl.

The woman laughed it off. "This is why I buy my souvenirs online and have them shipped to my house. Much easier and I get the best selection."

The girls nodded to each other as the woman turned back to the game. "That's a great idea!"

A couple of hours later, hot and worn out, they wanted a cold shower followed by a long nap but it was time to pack up their bags.

Except there was the small problem of their suitcases already being full of everything they'd brought with them. Now they had souvenirs from the museum and the ball park and they wanted to keep the beautiful program from the play.

"I'm not leaving anything here," Pearl said fiercely.

"Maybe we could mail some of these things to our houses?" Pepper speculated as she sat on the bulging suitcase while Pearl yanked on the zipper.

Pepper continued, "Next time we have to leave room for souvenirs or bring an extra suitcase just for things we buy."

Pearl's fingers ached as she tried to pull the zipper closed.

Pepper tenderly patted her sunburned nose. "Add sunscreen to our list. My nose is going to peel something awful."

"No more so than the blisters on my toes." Pearl grunted as she shoved hard on the corner of the suitcase.

"And for sure," Pepper continued really getting into her trip review. "When we go walking, we have to bring a bag to carry everything," she paused, "a large cross-body tote with extra-wide straps."

"We only wore two sets of clothes." As the zipper finally closed, Pearl fell back with relief. “Why did we bring all of this stuff?!” Beads of sweat popped up on her brow.

Triumphant, the girls half-carried half-dragged their suitcases out of the room. Their art posters were clamped tightly under their arms, baseball caps were lopsided on their heads. Pepper carried the city guide book and Pearl had a piece of paper sticking out of a pocket.

Travel Necessities:

Small camera
Small sketchpad, 1 pencil
Sunscreen
Bible
Walking shoes
Leave guidebook at home
Shampoo, soap …

In the lobby Pepper casually put the heavy guide book down on a table then walked away. Some other guest could enjoy it.

She joined their group loading onto the bus. It had been a fabulous trip.

Pearl & Pepper Make Repairs

When Pearl came in her bedroom she found Pepper up to her elbows in a large plastic bin.

All around her other bins were open; binders, construction paper of all colors some pieces cut up in shapes and scraps, swatches and folds of material were stacked up on the floor and bed.

“What are you doing?” Pearl’s forehead

furrowed in distaste at her cousin. "You're making a mess."

"There you are." Pepper spun around. "Where is the pattern for the sock puppets we made for the talent show last year? I want to make a set for a little girl who is sick but I can't find the patterns."

Pearl scanned the piles of craft books next to the boxes of supplies. "I would have thought that it was right here. Could it be at your house?"

"No," Pepper sighed, "I already looked there."

"Where did we get the pattern?"

"I don't know." Pepper flopped down on a chair. "I can't remember. I think we picked it up at a craft show."

Pearl searched her memory for the

pattern. "Let's go to the church and get the puppets then work from there."

"Can't. I called the coordinator. She said a few months after the show they found a leaky window. The box the puppets were in got wet and mildewed. They tossed the puppets and everything else in the box."

"Well, this isn't helping. Let's clean up this mess. Maybe you missed it when you were searching."

After two more days of hunting the girls were ready to give up. They had searched through closets, boxes of Christmas sweaters, swatches of fabric, craft supplies, half finished projects and other rooms of the house where the pattern could not possibly be.

One sitting on the porch swing, the other in a rocking chair, their clothes wrinkled, hair mussed, faces bushed, they watched their cousin Drake working in the yard.

"We may have to start from scratch."

"Let's find a different puppet. There's plenty of other instructions. We can make a new one," Pearl suggested.

"The little girl saw the play and wants the mountain climber character. I remember the character. I just can't remember all of the details for the face, hair, or clothes. Maybe once we get started, we'll remember more about it." Pepper sighed, "I guess it doesn't have to be perfect."

Drake paused and propped his elbow up on the handle of the rake. "Did anybody take pictures during the play? Maybe you can use those to make a new pattern?"

The girls looked at each other. Why

hadn't they thought of that? Pepper jumped up and hurried to the phone.

A week later as bits of material, glue, scissors, and sewing needles were scattered around the living room, the girls compared the new sock puppet to the pictures.

Pepper examined their work. The mountain climber puppet had weathered blue jean pants and a red scruffy shirt sewn onto the sock. He sported a climbing harness made of yarn. The face was painted on with brown eyes and brown yarn for hair.

"Well, it's not exactly the same but close enough." Pepper smiled, satisfied.

The kitchen phone rang as they were cleaning up.

"Yes?" Pearl dropped a leftover piece of material into a plastic bin. "Janet, hey."

She paused listening. "Sure, I remember the afghan. Oh really? That sounds horrible. Yeah, we can take care of it."

"What happened?" Pepper asked as she riffled the fridge for some leftovers.

"Janet dropped some gravy on her afghan. Her dog Lefty chewed on it damaging the corner. She wants a repair, if we can."

"No problem. Let's go over there tomorrow and pick it up. Tonight, I'm exhausted. Want some ham?" She carried a plate of leftover ham in one hand and a bowl of potato salad in the other. "Get the pitcher of tea and some glasses."

After school the next day the girls swung by Janet's house to pick up the afghan. Back at home they pulled out their yarn supplies but they didn't have the colors of the original. The afghan was a Christmas pattern that brought to mind poinsettias but didn't have any actual flowers.

"That's fine. I need to get some wool blend yarn anyway." Pearl was delighted to have any excuse to go to the craft shop.

In the yarn isle they surveyed the colors and picked some that looked right for the blanket, spending a happy hour among the rows of balls and skeins.

At home they compared the newly bought yarn with the afghan. "These colors don't match." Pearl was irritated. "I wanted to get this done today."

"We'll have to take the blanket to the store to match the colors directly." Pepper scowled.

Days later the girls found time to get back to the store. Each cousin held a side of the afghan, the far corner dragged the floor as they compared every green on every shelf, including thread from another brand.

"Even if the thread content or size doesn't match exactly," Pepper held up a ball of yarn next to the afghan, "we could make do but the color isn't close enough. Nothing works."

She glared at the rows of yarn. "Do you remember the name of the colors we used?"

Pearl frowned down at the afghan. "No, I can't remember. We made this a year ago. We may have to order the yarn to match these colors. We need to get the pattern so we'll know what we used."

Pepper's face fell. "We have to find this green or do something else with the corner." She thought for minute, fingers tracing the edge of the square. "I guess we could tie off the ends and put in a flower or just stitch in a complimentary color."

The glare Pearl gave the afghan was fierce. “It’ll look like a patch on a pair of pants.”

“Do you have a better suggestion?!” Pepper snapped. She tromped down the isle and plopped into a chair.

The store had work tables and chairs at the end of some rows. A woman standing at a nearby table had overheard their conversation. She had strips of a knitted work in front of her as she selected new yarns.

“Sounds like quite the predicament. ‘Been there myself. The companies make changes to colors all the time. Even if they made a new run of a particular color, it wouldn’t match exactly.”

“We only need a couple of feet,” Pearl wailed. She pulled out a chair and plopped down.

"Have you considered a yarn swap?" The woman asked.

Pepper and Pearl stared at the woman, minds racing. "That could work. When's the next craft show?"

"Wait a minute!" Pepper jumped in the air. "Sally made Christmas stockings out of this same green!"

While Pepper called Sally, Pearl admired the knitted strips that were to make a long vest the woman was working on. Before you know it, Pearl had made a copy of the pattern and was selecting a couple of coordinating colors that would work with yarn she had at home.

"We've got some!" Pepper shouted, to the amusement of a few other customers.

Back at home Sally had dropped off the yarn scraps and it was just a few minutes to fix the damaged square. Armed with chocolate milk and cookies the cousins surveyed the repaired blanket.

"Whew, it has been a tough couple of weeks." Pearl leaned back in the couch, tucking hair behind one ear, and propped her feet on the coffee table.

"We have to get organized," Pepper groaned.

"What we have to do is revise our repairs and duplicates policy." Pearl said firmly.

Pepper squinted a half-glare at her.

"I ain't doin' this again!" Pearl cried. "Once we finish a project that's it from now on. If you want to fix something or make another one, you're on your own."

Pepper wasn't willing to concede so easily. She was proud of her crafts and didn't mind a little extra work now and again.

"What we need is a binder to keep track of the patterns that we have used. We could take a picture of each project as we finish it. That would help." Pepper reasoned, ignoring her cousin's frustration.

"We've made dozens of crafts. There is no way that we can keep track of all of the patterns. A lot of them we modified to fit our projects." Pearl said between gulps of chocolate milk.

"And, we rarely use the same materials or colors from the pattern." Pepper selected a cookie.

The girls studied on it.

"We need a scrapbook." Pepper said as she thought it through.

"O.K." Pearl began wrapping her head around this idea. "If we take a picture and keep the pattern, we could glue them into a scrapbook."

"Then on one side of the page we could make notes of any changes that we make," Pepper speculated.

"It would be a bit of work at first."

"We could add a new page as we make each project."

"As long as we don't let it pile up."

"We could start with the stuff we're working on right now."

The girls looked at each other with a gleam in their eyes. They had a new project.

Pearl & Pepper
The Family Quilt

"Hurry up," Pepper pleaded. "You're taking forever! I want to get to the museum." She had a tote bag over one shoulder with a sketch pad sticking out the top.

"Don't worry," Pearl said with a teasing smile as she combed her hair. "The quilts will still be there. Let me get my camera and we'll race right over."

"This show only comes every two years.

I just can't wait to get there." Craft shows really inspired Pepper's love of handicrafts.

The quilts did not disappoint! The complexity and cleverness of the designs were fantastic. Some showed scenes of landscapes. Some were classic quilt blockings. One quilt was hundreds of tiny squares of cloth in similar colors blended together to make a face. Amazing.

The girls took pictures and sketched the designs. One quilt, about eight feet high and six feet wide, was made of little tiny squares of brown, yellow, and green that made a sunflower field.

For others the cousin crafters pressed their faces up close to examine stitching. On another they examined fabric choices that showed a red and white windmill pattern.

Later, in a nearby café the girls talked

about the magnificent quilts over grilled cheese sandwiches. One of their favorites had been the hand prints of all of the grandchildren in a family.

They were inspired.

"We should do a family quilt!" Pepper said, adventure lighting up her face.

Never ones to ignore opportunity, they flipped the paper menu over and began sketching ideas for a quilt that they could make.

"First," Pepper roughly sketched a grid of nine blocks, "we'll need a grid for our family."

Pearl counted family members. "Wait, were you thinking of one block for different family members?" She asked.

"Yes," Pepper said, looking down at the

grid she had drawn. “Oh, this grid won’t work.”

Quickly the girls counted all of the current family members. They arrived at the total about the same time.

“If we do one block for each adult family member,” Pearl thought a moment, “that would be almost 30 blocks. The quilt would have to be huge or I guess we could do really small blocks.” She looked at the nine block grid with dismay.

They crunched bites of grilled cheese as they thought about it. These 2nd cousins knew that anything could be accomplished with creativity.

Pearl wondered aloud, “What if we only did the older family members? You know, only the grandparents. Maybe later we could do the next generation?”

Pepper counted out the generations from their family. "That would be the greats, grandparents, parents, cousins, then Chance has a baby boy – would we have to do a quilt for him or wait for others from your generation to have kids?" This was getting complicated.

"What if we didn't? Would we hurt somebody's feelings?" Pearl asked.

"I don't think so," said Pepper. "We do crafts all the time. Every project doesn't have to be for every family member."

Pearl nodded as they cleaned up their table and headed for home.

The next afternoon they went back to the drawing board or rather Pepper's sketch pad. She drew designs as they talked.

"O.K." Pearl declared. "I don't see how we can include the greats but if we put the grandparents in the center then we can show the children branching out. That might work."

"But your grandmother is my aunt. Will we do two quilts?" Pepper sketched a larger center square surrounded by smaller squares.

Face pensive, Pearl doodled some names into the squares that Pepper was drawing. "Shall we just do a shape quilt like pinwheels or a star and embroider all our names in the blocks?"

Pepper roughly sketched one pinwheel block then scribbled lines to represent names. She looked up from her sketchpad. "I'd like to do something more interesting but I'm not sure how much work we want to put in it."

"How about a picture of some kind? Should we use stitching to reveal a design or maybe we could cut out shapes from fabric?" Pearl asked.

"I loved the look of the exhibit quilts but it seems really time consuming. What if we cut shapes out of different types of material? We could then sew them onto different background colors to make a scene. Like mountains or something." Pepper commented.

"What if, instead of a square per branch – we could do that another time – what if we did family scenes?" Pearl suggested.

"Scenes?" This was intriguing. "What kind of scenes?"

"Maybe we could use material to make a cabin."

"At the lake!"

Pearl nodded, eyes shining.

They reviewed their grid. Pearl picked up her notepad and began making a list of places and events that were special to their family.

At the fabric store the girls considered many different patterns and colors.

"How about a dark color, like navy blue, as the background?" Pearl asked.

"Hmm," Pepper pulled a bolt of cloth out of a rack. "Navy for a background? How are we going to show the scenery?" She pulled out another bolt of material. "How about something milder? Maybe soft linen white."

Pepper was more visually minded than Pearl. She pictured the quilt with different color combinations.

They tried matching several colors by laying them side by side. After much discussion they settled on colors for the background, the borders, and for the pieces of the scenes.

Back in Pearl's living room, the girls laid out the material that they had bought. Pepper flipped to a new page in her sketch pad.

"What family scenes do we want to show? The cabin for sure. It has been in the family for several years." She began sketching the outline of the cabin by the lake.

"What about great-grandpa's farm? All of the great aunts and uncles and your grandmother grew up there." Pearl said.

"I like it. What crops should we show in the field? Then there's the house with the porch swing and the barn. Should we squeeze in a few cows?" Pepper said. She surveyed a fabric that had printed scenes of barns and cows.

Pearl wasn't listening, she was pulling out photo albums. "What about fishing? You know everyone in the family loves the outdoors."

On and on the girls brainstormed all afternoon until they had a pile of ideas, more than enough for ten quilts.

A few days later, once again in Pearl's living room, they began working on piecing their ideas together. First, they laid out their paper drawings. Then Pearl taped several pieces of newsprint together until it was about the same size as the quilt would be.

Pepper placed the sketches she had drawn over the paper. There were a lot of them. There were pictures of fiddles, a cabin, a farm, bicycles, fishing poles, quilts, jigsaw puzzle pieces, a stack of books, a Christmas tree, and more.

They stared at the result. The whole newsprint was covered.

"This might be a little busy." Pearl said.

Pepper grinned. "Do you think so?"

They shared a laugh. "Maybe we should take out a few ideas. Let's pick the ones we like the most."

Pepper picked up a couple of drawings. "Let's weed out these."

It took some give and take but an hour later the girls had a group of scenes that they liked. They taped the pictures to the newsprint then got busy tracing out the scenes of the squares onto tracing paper.

"I'll cut out the individual pieces of the design," Pearl picked up a pair of scissors, "you mark up the fabrics."

Comparing her progress to a quilt

pattern, she made sure to draw the design large enough to leave room to sew it to the other pieces. With a chalk pencil she dotted along the edge where the stitches would be.

Pepper took the individual pieces and began selecting different cloth to go with each item. Next, she pinned the patterns to the fabric and cut out the design.

By the time the girls finished cutting out the pieces and matching them up to the squares it was late. They were tired and rumpled.

It was almost a week before they could get back to work on their quilt. Pepper unrolled the material they had picked for the quilt top's background and began pinning the cut-outs to it.

"It still looks a little full, to me." Pepper mused. Chalk marks showed the grid.

"Yeah, there is too much stuff in the farm square. But still," Pearl said, thinking, "it seems like something is missing."

Some squares had family events and some were locations. There was the cabin by the lake, they had the greats' farm, there was a square for fishing and another for the mountains; really the mountains were more like large rolling hills of trees.

Pepper surveyed their work. "It seems sort of impersonal. These scenes could fit almost any family." She was apprehensive for a moment. "More personal is more work. This is already a big project."

"No, no." Pearl said firmly, shaking her head. "We have to stop somewhere. Nine blocks, simple designs and a border. We have to keep it manageable." She returned to the scene pieces that she was pinning together.

Before long Pearl and Pepper were bending

over their sewing machine, sewing pieces together. They carefully double checked their measurements, compared the finished blocks to their sketches then laid the blocks out on the floor to verify the full size of the quilt.

Over several days the girls met to work on their quilt while ideas and family feelings kept swirling in Pepper's mind.

Early one morning Pepper came rushing in to Pearl's kitchen. "I've got it!"

Bleary-eyed and finger-sore Pearl wasn't so excited to see her cousin. She poured milk into a bowl of cereal.

"We'll have each person sign it!" Pepper delivered this with a flourish.

Mouth full of cereal, Pearl wasn't sure this was a good idea but her cousin was fantastic at visual crafts. She listened patiently as Pepper explained. They agreed that this would work well.

They contacted each family member telling them what was needed. A few days later they had the extra pieces. Delighted, they pressed on with their project.

When each block was sewn and stacked in a pile, they prepared thin strips of the border material that would connect the blocks. First, they sewed the blocks into rows of three scene blocks. Once they had three rows of three blocks, they then sewed the rows together and added the border to make the full face of the quilt.

"I'd forgotten how much work this is." Pepper said. She stretched her shoulders at the sewing machine. She lifted the corner edge of the quilt to admire the last of the stitching. "I'm exhausted."

Pearl was head down on the arm of a

chair, scraps of material under one leg, a needle cushion slipping from her hand, almost asleep. “What?!”

“We finished the top. Look at it!” Pepper beamed.

The next day they rolled up the quilt-top and took it to a local quilters group who sewed the backing, batting, and top together.

Then a final stitch design was sewn across and around each block with a special sewing machine. The girls watched intently to make sure that the stitches were applied just so.

Later they spread the quilt over Pepper’s bed to admire it. One block showed a small farm with a few cows cut from the patterned material; in the distance were a couple of rows of cotton. There was a small log cabin by a lake. Another showed two figures sitting on a pier fishing. Of course, there was one block of nothing but mountains of rolling hills of trees.

The center block was a mishmash of various sized hearts in different colors with signatures of family members on them. In the middle of that block was a simple understated cross. It was almost easy to miss until one realized that the hearts were surrounding the base of the cross.

"Gorgeous."
"Better than I imagined."
"I love quilts."
"You can make anything into a quilt."

For a few seconds it was perfect.

Then Pepper thought of something. "If this is a family quilt—,"

"Yeah, family." Pearl nodded with satisfaction.

"Who gets it?"

Pearl & Pepper Crossword Crochet

"Christmas is coming." Pearl said, flipping through a knitting pattern book. As usual the 2nd cousins were lounging in Pearl's living room. Several knitting and crochet books and well-used magazines were piled up around her.

Pepper laid down her pencil then raised her eyebrows. "In six months. Are you thinking of shopping early?"

"Glory asked me to make her an afghan."

"Ooh, I adore afghans. Knitting or crochet?" Pepper asked.

"She didn't say but I've looked through all of our pattern books and there isn't anything that I love for her." She tossed the book onto the floor.

"Just use different styles of stitch patterns for each block, like a sampler," Pepper suggested. "That way the afghan will be unique to you."

"Oh, I don't know." Pearl sighed. "How are you doing on your puzzle?"

"It's harder making the clues than I thought and I still have to block out the grid." Pepper chewed on the edge of her pencil.

She was working on a personalized crossword puzzle for their cousin Cassie's birthday.

Pearl looked over her cousin's shoulder. Her face lit up. She loved puzzles. They both did. She pulled open a desk drawer.

"Can I help?! All we need is some graph paper. We'll write the answers out in a list then we'll match up the letters that are the same." Pearl suggested.

After trying to write the words in a way that crossed some of the letters the girls were getting frustrated. Their grid paper had letters up and down, some scratched out, other letters were squished in around marked-through places. It was a mess.

Pepper picked up a copy of the crossword from the local newspaper hoping for a clue as to how they did it.

"What about this, let's write each word going across then write them going down. We can cut them out in strips."

They began writing some words that they thought they might use for answers. Things that described Cassie or that she liked.

Dogs
Sparkly
Books
Jazz
Cousin
Princess
Dancing
Sister
Games
Fireworks

"Now," Pepper said. "Let's slide the words around until we get some of the words crossing each other somewhere."

The girls worked almost an hour sliding the words around until several letters of different words overlapped. Pearl grabbed a roll of tape and quickly taped the strips of words going across and down to a piece of graph paper.

"Excellent!" Pepper's eyes gleamed. "Now, I can fill in the gaps with gray squares."

Pearl studied the puzzle laid out on the graph paper. "Hmm, I wonder if I could do something similar with an afghan?"

Pepper looked up. "You mean use graph paper to plan a design. Great idea."

"I meant the puzzle. Maybe I could make a puzzle in the afghan pattern."

Pepper thought that seemed awfully complicated. "What kind of puzzle?"

"We could use a grid to map out squares." Pearl was already in her own world, brow furrowed, biting her lip.

"You are thinking of a crossword puzzle?

Many afghan patterns are a series of blocks, just like quilts. I guess it does lend itself to a grid format. You'd have to keep it simple."

Beginning to get excited Pearl grabbed a piece of graph paper then used the grid lines to trace a large square.

Pepper looked at the puzzle she had been working on for several days. "First we need to think of clues and answers. How many answers do you want to do?"

Pearl studied the paper puzzle they had just assembled. "We could use a basic crochet square pattern, like a granny square, in two colors. One color could be for the answers and another color would just fill out the grid."

She used a ruler to draw three lines across and three lines down.

Pepper continued, "I used things that Cassie likes; favorite flower, name of her dog – like that. How are you going to include the clues?"

"I'm not sure about clues yet but for the colors instead of just two, what if we used different colors for across and down. Crossing blocks could be a third color then the background or blank squares would be a fourth. It would make the afghan more visually interesting."

"Yeah," Pepper said, getting into the swing of creating something new. "To the casual observer it wouldn't be obvious that it's a crossword puzzle. Only Glory would know the secret."

"You might use different crochet stitch patterns for the squares for down and across. That could really make the overall design bolder." Pepper suggested.

Pearl got up. "Let's go to the yarn store and I'll think about words to put in the grid."

At the yarn store the girls mixed and matched several colors.

"I guess we could use basic gray or beige for the background." Pearl said.

"Do you know Glory's favorite color? You could use variations of it for the answers. Light, medium, and dark."

They laid different colors next to each other to see how they looked together. Holding up a skein Pepper said, "Look at this, you could use a variegated color for intersecting blocks."

Pearl grinned, "I love it. Glory loves peaches. Let's try a peaches-and-cream color grouping."

Back at home Pearl got busy writing out everything she knew about Glory.

Daughter - Whitley
Likes summer
Birthday in January

Favorite foods – sweet potatoes, peaches
Pastimes – puzzles, cooking
Favorite book…

The list continued on down the page.

Pearl then began trying to match up words. By the time she was called to supper she was weary and frustrated. Nothing seemed to work. Though she could match up some words, others just would not fit.

Tamping down on her frustration, she thought, *this is why I do this kind of thing. It challenges my creativity and skills. I'll figure it out.*

Over the next few days, she tried one thing after another. Nothing seemed to give the puzzle a feel or fancy that appealed to her. The message just wasn't right.

At school recess Pearl sat with a paper and pencil. While her mom shopped at the grocery store, she was leaning against a rack thinking of crisscrossing words. On a park bench in the rain, she balanced an umbrella over her paper and pencil trying to make portions of letters fit into a grid.

"I'm so disappointed," she told Pepper a few days later as they mixed up biscuits for supper. "I feel foiled." She momentarily grinned at her wordplay. "I wanted this blanket to be great."

Pepper patted her on the shoulder. "Don't give up. Take a step back and look at it from a different angle. Glory is coming for supper. Ask her questions about herself and see what comes to you."

"It's not just the pattern. How am I going to give her the clues? Just hand her a piece of paper? That would be sloppy."

Pepper thought for a minute. "How about if we write the clues in calligraphy on pretty paper? That would look good. Ooh," she had an idea. "What if you framed the clues to hang up on her wall? When she wants to change the picture on the wall, she can stick the clues page into a photo album."

"That would work. Sure. It would be attractive and classy. Yeah, let's do that," Pearl said, then groaned. "I still don't know what to do about the clues and answers. Maybe I should do a regular pattern for the afghan and try this idea another time." Her forehead wrinkled with worry.

Pepper was concerned. Crafts were supposed to be challenging but fun. "Cousin, I think you're over-thinking it."

Pearl threw her an annoyed sneer. "I want this to be special."

"Special doesn't mean complicated." Pepper tossed over her shoulder as she put the biscuits in the oven.

It was while watching Glory at supper that evening, around the table with several family members, that Pearl realized her dearest cousin was right. Simple was the way to go. She could barely wait for the table to be cleaned up so that she could get back to it.

Now when she hunched over her pencil and paper in her bedroom she giggled as she thought of ideas. In the park she turned her face up to the sky in thought. At lunch in the café Pepper read a book while Pearl jotted ideas.

Finally, Pearl had a number of words that were exactly what she wanted. She met Pepper in her room. "I did it. I've got some words." She held up a piece of grid paper with strips of words glued to the page, face beaming. "I even have a theme, 'Name your blessings.'"

"That's a lovely idea. Glory will like it. Now that we have answers and a puzzle design, let's make up the clues." Pepper said. "Then I'll write them out is calligraphy on creamy paper. I think I have a peach marker somewhere."

The next afternoon the cousins got busy with yarn and crochet hook. In a few days they had several squares in each of the four colors.

That weekend Pepper rushed into Pearl's room. "Ready to assemble?" She loved this part.

"Let's lay it all out on the floor to make sure we've got all of the pieces in the right order. Once it's whip-stitched together it'll be hard to fix mistakes."

They paced the pieces out on the floor, consulting the pattern frequently. Their faces smiling in delight and triumph of achievement, they stitched the squares together then crocheted a border.

The cousins couldn't wait to see what Glory would think of their gift.

When Christmas finally came Glory pulled the afghan from the box and stretched it out admiring the color combinations. "This is beautiful! I will snuggle up with it tonight."

The blank squares were a cream color, down squares were a rosy peach, across squares an orangey peach, and squares that crossed up and down were variegated of all three colors.

As Glory looked at the lovely blanket her eyes narrowed studying the pattern closely then a smile beamed in surprise. "It's a puzzle!"

The girls laughed with delight handing over the framed clues. "Yep. Have fun solving it."

Glory caught her breath. "My, my. Girls you are a blessing."

A Gift For Glory
Name Your Blessings

<u>Across</u>

1. Favor, anoint, gift
2. Belongs to you
3. Residence, where you rest and play
4. Admires you, crafter, beloved

<u>Down</u>

1. Relatives, abounds in love
2. Savior, redeemer, forgiver
3. A blessing to all, loved, appreciated
4. Cherish, wells up in your heart, is given freely

	1			2			3					
										4		
1						2			3			
		4										

A Gift For Glory
Name Your Blessings

	[1]F			[2]J			[3]G					
	A			E			L					
	M			S			O					
	I			U			R			[4]L		
[1]B	L	E	S	S		[2]M	Y		[3]H	O	M	E
	Y									V		
		[4]P	E	A	R	L				E		

Pearl & Pepper The Letter Challenge

"What are you doing with those?" Pearl came into the living room carrying a tray of iced tea and banana sandwiches.

Pepper was on the couch, reading a faded old letter from a bundle tied with blue ribbon.

"Grandma Grace mentioned writing letters with her aunt when she was a girl.

She loaned me these to read for myself. Be careful, don't drip anything on them."

Pepper carefully folded the letter and slipped it back into the bundle. "A friend and I used to exchange letters after she moved away. I've got them stashed in a keepsake box so I can read them again when I'm older. I really enjoyed having a pen pal."

"You don't write anymore?"

"No, we both got too busy." Pepper shrugged.

Seeing the stack of letters, "They must have written a lot." Pearl dropped down on the couch and took a sip of tea.

"There weren't telephones and cars to zip over to each other's houses back then. Writing was the only way to keep in touch." Pepper picked up a sandwich.

Later Pepper had the letters strewn around her while Pearl knitted by the window. She read one with a slight grin.

"Nobody writes letters anymore," Pepper said thoughtfully. "These are her thoughts, her style, her personality."

Putting down her knitting, Pearl sighed. "It seems like everything personal is vanishing. Now it's all store-bought cards, texts, and smiley faces. I miss those notes that showed one's manner and character. Wish we could do something about it."

As she gathered up the letters Pepper noticed her great aunt's handwriting. "Look at this."

Pearl leaned forward with a curious grin. The letters started out neat and clean but soon had scratched out words, scribbles along the edge of the paper, and extra words scrunched in between lines.

With a fond smile Pepper said, "I love the way she told a story. If she forgot a detail, she would just scribble it in wherever it would fit. I wish we had letters from the Greats."

As she considered this sentiment Pearl packed up her knitting. Then her face took on a certain expression. "You know, dear cousin, we might be able to do something after all."

Eyes alert, Pepper's eyebrow lifted in a question mark. "You've got the look! What!? Oh, we could call all the Greats and ask them to give us copies of their letters from when they were young," she exclaimed.

Pepper began to pace, fingers tapping her cheek as she began to formulate—

"No, no," Pearl interjected. "Old letters are fine for another day. What I want are brand new letters. Just for us!"

Spinning to a halt Pepper gave Pearl her

attention. Her 2nd cousin didn't always make sense—at first—but give her some time and you'd see her brilliant mind sparkle.

"New letters?" She asked.

The look had morphed into full-on excitement but Pepper wasn't understanding quite yet.

"I guess we could ask them to write us a letter," she ventured cautiously.

"Ask? Asking won't be enough," Pearl mumbled as she searched for a notebook. "They won't do it on their own."

"But we can't stand over their shoulder. Maybe we could ask them to reply to letters from us. I mean, if we pestered them—I doubt that would work. They are old and independent."

Pearl agreed. Nobody was going to order the Greats to do anything.

Over the next few days, the girls read articles on inspiration and motivation and manipulation.

"We could beg, bribe, or badger," Pepper suggested, "but I don't see either of those working."

Pearl had been turning this problem over in her mind for days. She came to a conclusion.

"We'll have to challenge them."

"A challenge! Oh, that's good. We can give them a prize or something, maybe a homemade—"

"No," Pearl shook her head with impatience. "No. Let's make it a competition." There was a fantastical gleam in her eye.

"You lost me. A competition?"

"We've got to do something that will

ensure they send us letters. We'll need to make it worth their while." Pearl began scribbling in her notebook.

Frustrated, Pepper glared. "But you said no prizes."

"Pepper, we are going to challenge their egos." Pearl delivered this with a waggle of her eyebrows.

For a moment Pepper didn't get it and then she did. The Greats, as the Youngers called them, had stiff egos where their siblings were concerned. A chuckle bubbled up from her chest.

"You are suggesting we challenge them to out-do each other?"

"Yep! Let's DARE them to out-do each other. One letter each month for a whole year!"

Laughing, Pepper could just imagine the Greats trying to come up with something better than the others were writing. She began working on a few ideas. "O.K. let's see, we could give them a topic each month, ask for their memories, and such."

Pearl nodded, a grin twitching her cheeks. "I love it. When can we start?"

And so, as was their habit, the girls got right to work.

Later, lounging in the living room Pearl stretched her legs from chair to coffee table. Crossing her ankles and fluttering her toes, she asked. "How do we maximize this opportunity?"

Not certain how to do so Pepper returned to the basics of the problem, or rather, the project. "What is our goal here? Getting them to all write the same Bible verse would be a nice handwriting comparison, I suppose."

Pepper continued, "Or details about

themselves? If we do convince the Greats to write us letters, what do we want from them?"

"Hmm." Pearl scrunched her toes. "Greatest moment in their lives? Day of their wedding? First moments when children were born?" She linked her hands behind her head, deep in thought. "Really, we could ask anything."

"Yeah, but what will make them do it? Let's just start with what we want them to write about. Are we going with twelve? Twelve topics for twelve months?"

"How about eleven and one freebie? They can pick one month to write about anything they want to."

Over the next few days there was a flurry of ideas. What would be enough to challenge the Greats? What did they want to know about the Greats' lives; their thoughts, opinions, triumphs?

Slips of paper floated to the floor as Pearl scribbled questions and ideas on page after page. Pepper spent some time flying paper air planes covered in cartoon drawings.

“This project seems more difficult than most others.” Pepper said. “I don’t want to send out a questionnaire that the Greats fill in. They won’t go for that.”

“I want to see their viewpoints, their personalities, their experiences, their wisdom. I want to hear about their follies,” declared Pearl.

It seemed the challenge in this project was on them. It was while they were reading articles on interviewing people for a media class that they had a stroke of blessing. Ask questions that had to be answered with an explanation.

That began one of their famous lists.

The Letter Challenge

Tell me a story, some of it should be true.
What do you collect?
Why were you born?
If you were someone else, who would you be?
Describe a magnificent year.
Write your life story in the words of a relative.
What will be your first words to God in Heaven?
Predict the rest of your life.
Funniest moment of your life.
God's blessings to you.
Freebie—writer's choice.
Greatest effort toward a goal.
A perfect moment.
When did you make the best of a situation?
If you could not die, how would you live?
If God gave you three choices, what would they be?
Which fork in the road did you take?
What will be said about you?

In the end the girls decided to give the

Greats the whole list of questions and topics and let them choose. Then came the hard part.

Convincing them to do it.

They brainstormed ideas for days. A singing telegram. Monogrammed invitations. Withholding their latest artistic creations. A fancy tea party to put them in a generous mood.

Wheedling was tossed early on along with begging and cajoling. On and on they worked until they had crafted a plan. They had to challenge their big egos and they would have to do it when they were all together or it wouldn't work.

At a family gathering a few weeks later they got their chance.

"I've been thinking of starting a pen

pal group," Pearl began casually, as if just making conversation.

"You know, Uncle Loch, I hear you're the best writer of the Greats." She tossed this line out like a lure on a fishing pole.

Pepper joined in. "Auntie Ossie, aren't you the funniest of your brothers and sister?"

"Now, wait just a minute," sputtered Lleu.

"Hey, I've been known to—"

"Don't start that," frowned Elwick. "You all know that I am the best jokester in this family."

In short order the Greats were boasting to each other about their various talents. The girls shared a smile as they watched their elder relatives fussing amongst themselves.

They just might get those letters after all.

Note to Readers

Pearl and Pepper, hereby, challenge all adults to write a letter to the children in your life every month for one year. Give your children something to cherish alongside their memories.

We further, hereby, challenge all children to write a letter or draw a picture for the greats in your life.

Leave an echo of your life.
Write a letter today.